"Have A Nice Evening?"
Jake Inquired.

With gritted teeth, he reminded himself that Rebecca's last-minute date with a guy from the suburbs was only an act of rebellion. Even so, he had waited up for her.

"Very nice," Rebecca informed him.

His hands were jammed into the back pockets of his jeans as if they had to be restrained from reaching out and shaking her. "Known the guy long?"

Rebecca's chin lifted, and mutinous anger glinted in her blue eyes. "What are you? My keeper?"

"No. I plan on being your lover. You might as well get used to the idea."

"That's not an idea," she retorted, infuriated. "It's a delusion!"

Dear Reader:

Welcome! You hold in your hand a Silhouette Desire—your ticket to a whole new world of reading pleasure.

A Silhouette Desire is a sensuous, contemporary romance about passions, problems and the ultimate power of love. It is about today's woman—intelligent, successful, giving—but it is also the story of a romance between two people who are strong enough to follow their own individual paths, yet strong enough to compromise, as well.

These books are written by, for and about every woman that you are—wife, mother, sister, lover, daughter, career woman. A Silhouette Desire heroine must face the same challenges, achieve the same successes, in her story as you do in your own life.

The Silhouette reader is not afraid to enjoy herself. She knows when to take things seriously and when to indulge in a fantasy world. With six books a month, Silhouette Desire strives to meet her many moods, but each book is always a compelling love story.

Make a commitment to romance—go wild with Silhouette Desire!

Best,

Isabel Swift
Senior Editor & Editorial Coordinator

CATHIE LINZ
Change of Heart

Silhouette Desire

Published by Silhouette Books New York

America's Publisher of Contemporary Romance

SILHOUETTE BOOKS
300 East 42nd St., New York, N.Y. 10017

Copyright © 1988 by Cathie L. Baumgardner

ISBN: 0-373-05408-4

First Silhouette Books printing February 1988

America's Publisher of Contemporary Romance

Printed in the U.S.A.

CATHIE LINZ

was in her mid-twenties when she left her career in a university law library to become a full-time writer of contemporary romantic fiction. In the six years since then, this Chicago author has had a dozen romances published. An avid world traveler, she often uses humorous mishaps from her own trips as inspiration. Still, she's always glad to get back home to her two cats, her trusty word processor and her hidden cache of Oreo cookies!

In Loving Memory
of
my father
and
his unfailing sense of humor, and
with much gratitude to those who
helped me through
the
hard times.

Special thanks to Alison Hart
(aka Jennifer Greene),
a talented writer and a special friend!

One

Jake Fletcher impatiently jabbed the elevator call button for what felt like the twentieth time. He'd been in Washington, D.C., for only a few hours, and already he was tense. Coming back might not have been a good idea, but he couldn't keep running from the memories forever. After all, he had lived and worked here for six years of his life. Then something had happened that made him question everything.

The result had been burnout—a common enough occurrence for a cop, or so he'd been told. But accepting it was something else. He still had a hard time believing it was three years since he'd turned in his badge.

Muttering a curse, Jake turned his back on the antiquated elevator. The tactic apparently worked; a second later he heard the soft bell proclaiming its arrival. But before he could turn around, he heard something else.

"Don't move!" The command was curt and imperative.

Jake froze, his muscles taut as he braced himself for trouble. His police training was too deeply ingrained to be forgotten. Within seconds he had checked his surroundings, noted the exits and established that the hotel hallway was completely deserted. Looking around with narrowed hazel eyes, he checked the interior of the elevator, but it, too, appeared to be empty.

"You're getting paranoid," Jake muttered to himself in disgust. And he was going to miss that elevator if he didn't hurry.

Moving quickly to prevent its departure, he thrust his arm against the elaborately decorated elevator doors. The gilded grillwork shrank back as if it had an aversion to him, and he heard the voice again.

"I'm serious! Don't come any closer!"

He'd heard of talking vending machines, but a talking elevator? Gathering his startled thoughts, Jake realized that this particular voice had a very human source. The orders were coming from a woman who was down on her hands and knees, squinting at the elevator's less than inspiring carpeting. She was located in the corner to the left of the doors, which was why he hadn't seen her sooner.

She repeated her earlier warning. "Don't come any closer!"

"Are you hurt, in trouble, what?" Tension made him brusque.

"I've lost my contact lens," she informed him.

Jake laughed at himself and his automatic assumption of danger. Talk about jumping at shadows!

Rebecca de Witt momentarily abandoned her search to look up and give the man a resentful glare. Personally, she didn't see anything amusing about her present situation; she couldn't see anything, period!

Rebecca closed her nonfocusing left eye to get better vision from the remaining contact lens in her right eye. The maneuver screwed up her face too much for her to sustain it long, but she did get a brief impression of a tall man with dark hair. Now that he'd stopped laughing he appeared to be staring at her. She supposed it was pretty strange to find someone on her knees in an elevator, but something told her that wasn't the reason for his fascination.

She was right. Looking down, Rebecca was dismayed to discover that her pose transformed her elegant black dress into something worthy of a *Playboy* layout. The normally reasonable neckline was gaping alarmingly, showing far more flesh than was decent.

Jake was disappointed when she placed a protective hand over the dress's scooped neckline. He'd enjoyed the tantalizing view of creamy skin and shadowy cleavage. His attention shifted to her face, where he noted the grim set of her full lips before focusing on her squinting eyes. If looks could kill, Jake thought to himself with amusement, he'd be six feet under right now.

"I'd appreciate it if you'd take another elevator." Her voice was colder than permafrost.

"And leave you here all alone on the floor to fend for yourself? I wouldn't dream of it." Jake had a feeling he'd dream of her, though. She was that kind of woman. Classy. A dark-haired Grace Kelly. And what gorgeous hair it was—chestnut-colored, smooth as silk, and so long that it fell well past her shoulders. This elevator might have been worth the long wait after all, he decided with a predatory smile.

Even though Rebecca couldn't see the smile, she sensed trouble. Holding out her hand in a deterring gesture, she firmly said, "Really, I don't need any help." She didn't want an audience for her awkward search. And she certainly didn't want this man seeing any more of her than he already had. "I'll have a much better chance of spotting the lens by myself."

"I find that hard to believe."

Rebecca found her entire evening hard to believe. She'd run into one snag after another. Normally she was a fairly competent woman, able to deal with being a single parent, able to manage on her limited budget. Yet here she was, brought to her knees by a stupid contact lens! Feeling at a definite disadvantage, she struggled to get to her feet, but a strong hand on her shoulder stopped her. The man had joined her in the elevator.

Obviously not the type who took orders well, Rebecca noted caustically. Which, in her experience with men, usually meant that he was the type who *gave* orders. She was right.

"Don't get up on my account." His command was issued in a sexy drawl. "I wouldn't want you stepping on your contact lens."

"You're probably already stepping on it!" Rebecca retorted as the elevator doors closed, sealing them both inside.

"Maybe it's not on the floor. Maybe it fell on your dress. Did you consider that?" Jake inquired with mock helpfulness.

"Yes, I considered that. And I already checked my dress."

"Too bad," he murmured. "I would have volunteered for the job."

"Is that supposed to be a compliment?" she countered.

"Yes."

His ready admission threw her. She had a sinking feeling that this man was a master of the unexpected. As the slow-moving elevator finally began its descent to the next floor, Rebecca tried to piece together a mental picture of him. Right now he was merely a shadowy blur to her. He appeared to be quite tall, but then, from her present perspective, even a Munchkin would seem tall. His voice was disturbingly masculine, deep and somewhat gritty. The voice of a man who had a dark side to him.

But speculating about this stranger was not going to help her find her contact lens, and that was her number-one priority. It had to be here somewhere. Keeping one hand on the recalcitrant neckline of her dress, Rebecca ran her other hand over the diamond-patterned carpeting.

Jake watched her for a moment or two. He liked the look of her, the graceful way she moved. He wanted to see more of her; he wanted to see all of her. Without the black dress. Wearing nothing but that golden locket that hung between her breasts. The suddenness and intensity of the attraction surprised him.

"Show me where you dropped this contact," he ordered somewhat tersely.

Rebecca resented his high-handed approach. "If I knew where I dropped it, I wouldn't still be looking for it."

"Touchy, touchy."

"You do and you'll be sorry," she muttered under her breath.

Jake heard the comment and laughed. It was a long time since a woman had made him laugh. He'd almost forgotten the feeling.

The closeness of his laughter made Rebecca even more uneasy. He was suddenly kneeling barely a foot away from her. She still couldn't see him clearly, but she suspected he was looking at her instead of searching for her contact lens.

This situation was becoming much too bizarre, she decided. Here she was, on a hotel elevator floor, with some pushy man she'd never met before.

Just as she was about to call off the search, he suddenly exclaimed, "Wait, I think I see it!"

"Where?" she demanded.

"Over there."

He pointed, but all she could see was his hand. It was a surprisingly appealing hand. His lean fingers gave her the impression of strength and sensitivity. Startled by the personal direction of her thoughts, she shifted nervously.

"No, don't move," he cautioned her. "Stay right there. I'll get it."

He inched closer and leaned across her, his arm outstretched as if he were reaching for something. His shoulder brushed hers, and she shivered. Yet she wasn't cold; she was warm. Very warm. And he was making her warmer. Heat spread through her, originating at the point where his shoulder had inadvertently touched hers.

Her response confused and disturbed her. He was so close that his breath glanced off her face, stirring the loose strands of her long hair. She couldn't breathe, couldn't think. This rush of excitement was unexpected and uncontrollable.

As if reading her thoughts, he paused. She could almost feel him looking at her. She closed her eyes and tried to hang on to her composure. But her other senses overcompensated for her lack of sight. She could smell the tantalizing aroma of masculine soap, feel the uneven pounding of her heart, hear him inhale sharply.

He was going to kiss her. She knew it. Her logical mind protested, but her body remained frozen, waiting, anticipating. Rebecca was so caught up in the moment that she was unaware of the elevator stopping or the gilded doors opening. Jake was equally distracted.

They were brought back to earth by a child's high-pitched voice. "What are those two people doing on the floor, Mommy?"

The question was followed by a woman's horrified exclamation. "Close your eyes, children!"

Rebecca opened her eyes and stared in dismay at the group waiting for the elevator.

"I've never seen such disgraceful behavior!" the woman sniffed.

"Too bad, you're missing a lot," Jake couldn't resist murmuring.

As the elevator doors began to close, Rebecca scrambled to her feet, not caring if she stepped on her missing lens or not.

Jake moved quickly to save the contact lens from certain destruction. "Watch out!"

But Rebecca wasn't about to fall for the same line twice. "You're the one I should have been watching out for!" she retorted while angrily punching the Open Door button. The elevator ignored her and resumed its lumbering descent.

"Are you upset because I almost kissed you, or because we were interrupted?"

Outrage stiffened her spine. "I can assure you that I'm not the kind of woman who appreciates having strangers kiss me in an elevator."

"No?" He was clearly intrigued. "Then where do you appreciate having strangers kiss you?"

Rebecca stoically ignored him and his provocative question. Confidence was obviously not a problem with this man. He had an answer for everything.

Rebecca wished she had a few answers herself. Why hadn't she backed away from him? Why hadn't she resisted more? Why hadn't she resisted even a little?

"Don't you want your contact lens?" His question was directed to her back, since she refused to turn around.

"Not if you're going to hassle me, no." Her words had sharp edges.

"I'm not going to hassle you." Taking her hand, he unclenched her fingers from the fist she'd made and carefully placed the contact lens in her palm. As promised, he immediately released her.

"Aren't you going to say thank-you?" he prompted in an amused voice as the elevator finally reached the ground floor.

She remained silent until the doors were open. After stepping into the safety of the lobby, Rebecca took a deep breath and decided she could afford to be courteous. "Thank you."

"You could thank me by having a drink with me," he immediately countered. "Or how about dinner?"

This man was obviously on the prowl, but she wasn't about to become the prey. "No, thank you," she refused politely. "Goodbye."

"Wait a minute." He blocked her escape. "Where are you going?"

"To put in my lens. I'm tired of squinting." She calmly stepped around him and continued on her way.

Jake watched her walk away. He'd forgotten that she wasn't able to see him. Talk about blind dates! He smiled as he saw her pause on the other side of the lobby and squint at the sign on the washroom door before she pushed the door open and disappeared inside.

He had no intention of giving up. This classy lady intrigued him, and he wasn't about to let her get away.

Unaware of the man waiting outside, Rebecca soaked her lens in cleaning solution, returned it to its rightful place and studied her reflection in the mirror. She could see again. Hallelujah!

She wasn't sure she liked what she saw, however. Her hair was mussed, her cheeks flushed. Out came the hairbrush, the cinnamon-colored lipstick, the face powder for the shiny spot on her nose, and repairs were quickly made.

There, that was better. She nodded approvingly. Now that she was standing up, the neckline of her dress had resumed its proper place, thank goodness. She straightened the gold locket that held a picture of her three-year-old daughter, Amy.

Rebecca checked the time on her slim gold wristwatch. Amy would be in bed by now. Dorothy, the family housekeeper, would already have tucked her in. Dorothy had done the same for Rebecca as a young girl. The older woman had been more surrogate mother than housekeeper, helping Rebecca through the bumpy years of early adolescence and the temperamental giddiness of her teens.

Unfortunately, there wasn't time to dwell on pleasant memories. If she wanted to make it to the Women in Careers banquet before it began, she'd better get moving.

The possibility that the man who'd almost kissed her in the elevator would be waiting for her in the lobby never occurred to Rebecca. It should have, she realized. He wasn't the kind of man to give up easily.

As he turned to face her, she saw him clearly for the first time and recognized him immediately. She'd never met him before today, but she'd seen his photograph often enough to identify him—Jake Fletcher. Suspense writer extraordinaire. Former Washington, D.C., police officer, former student in her father's creative writing class, now her father's special dinner guest for this evening.

Jake Fletcher looked more experienced, more dangerous than his photographs implied. His face was angular. Deep lines fanned from the corners of his eyes, eyes that were dark and full of shadows. She was too far away to discern their color—hazel or brown—but there was no mistaking their expression. Jake was eyeing her with blatant interest.

Deliberately avoiding his gaze, Rebecca covertly studied the rest of him. Tall and lean, he emanated the high-powered tension of a man always on the move. She guessed his height to be an inch or two more than six feet. She already knew his age—thirty-three—which made him five years older than she.

Beneath the civilizing confines of a dark suit, white shirt and charcoal-gray tie was an unmistakable toughness that success hadn't tempered. This was a man who lived by his own rules and wouldn't conform to anyone else's.

That jibed with what her father had told her about Jake Fletcher, the only student of his to have made it really big. That was three years ago, and Rebecca had been living in Chicago then, but her father's letters had been full of stories about his favorite pupil.

At the time, Jake's job as an undercover police officer had fascinated her father, who was an avid reader of suspense novels. He and Jake had discussed various authors and shared a common complaint about the implausibility of a particular best-selling novel. Jake's claim that he could write a better book had proved to be true. According to her father, Jake had the natural talent of a streetwise storyteller. A year and a half later Jake's first novel had been published to much critical acclaim. The commercial success of his second book, released early this spring, had quickly established him as a popular author.

Although she'd never admit it to her father, Rebecca had read both of Jake's books. His heroes were tough he-men who believed women were disposable commodities. Loners who never let anything get in the way of their assignments, they succeeded whatever the cost. Given his police background, she suspected that the author was very much like his fictional protagonists.

But what was Jake doing here? He was supposed to be having dinner at home with her father tonight, not hanging around a hotel lobby trying to pick her up!

"I hope that strange look on your face means you can see again," Jake said.

"I can see." That didn't mean that what she saw pleased her, however.

"Then how about telling me your name." His comment was more command than request.

"Rebecca. And you're Jake Fletcher." She made it sound like an accusation.

"That's right." Jake assumed she recognized him from the late-night talk show he'd recently done, one of the few promotional appearances he'd agreed to. "Now that we've got the introductions out of the way, how about reconsidering my dinner invitation?"

Rebecca's anger grew. "I can't believe you've got the nerve to invite me to have dinner with you!"

"If you knew me better, you'd realize that I've got plenty of nerve."

"Nerve but no memory," she retorted. "You're supposed to be having dinner with my father this evening!"

Jake looked confused. "Your father?"

"That's right. My father, Bill de Witt. For the past two weeks he's talked of nothing but how his prize student, Jake Fletcher, was coming to dinner tonight. Tonight, Sunday night, the third of May," she reiterated. "My father has had Dorothy cooking up a storm all day just for you. And here you are, blithely handing out dinner invitations without giving him a second thought!"

Wanting to verify her identity, Jake didn't bother denying her accusation. "Wait a second. Let me get this straight. You're Bill's daughter?"

"That's right."

"Bill's daughter...the librarian?" Jake shook his head in amazement while his eyes moved over her, from her shapely legs all the way up to her recently glossed lips. "Funny, you don't look like a librarian."

Rebecca knew from reading Jake's last novel that he stereotyped librarians as dried-up prunes, but at the moment she was more concerned about her personal privacy than her profession's image problem. There was only one way Jake could have known that she was a librarian: from her father. And that thought brought up other disturbing possibilities. "What else did my father tell you about me?"

Jake was wondering the same thing himself. What else *had* Bill told him in those long, amusing letters of his? Jake ruefully admitted that he hadn't paid much attention to Bill's occasional references to his family. A loner himself, the subject of family matters hadn't interested him very much. But now he found that Rebecca interested him very much indeed.

So he made a solid effort to remember. Wait . . . Jake frowned. Hadn't Bill mentioned something about a grandchild? Rebecca's child? Or her brother's? Was she married? He'd automatically checked her ring finger as soon as he'd entered the elevator. No ring. She wore no jewelry at all other than a watch and that gold locket.

More snippets of Bill's letters came back to him. She *had* been married but now was . . . what? Divorced? Or had she been left a widow?

"What else did my father tell you?" Rebecca repeated angrily.

Jake wished he could remember but, seeing how defensive she was, decided not to say anything about her past until he'd confirmed the facts with Bill. He suspected it would be easier to get information from Rebecca's father than from her. "Your father didn't tell me much. He certainly didn't tell me he was sending you to pick me up."

"I didn't come to pick you up." She said the words as if they were distasteful.

"Then what are you doing here? I thought you were supposed to be joining us for dinner tonight."

"You and my father will be eating alone. I've got other plans this evening," Rebecca replied, infinitely glad that she'd made it a *point* to have other plans. Jake was the latest in a string of bachelors her father had paraded in front of her since she'd moved back to Washington six months ago. She loved her father dearly, but she wasn't about to sit still for his continual matchmaking. "You're already late," she reminded Jake. "You should have been there fifteen minutes ago."

"Your father knows about the change in plans. I just called him."

"You'd better not have canceled."

Jake was silent for a moment as he noted the passion in her voice. Rebecca might look cool, but obviously the composure was only skin-deep. He noticed with amusement that she'd attempted to erase any outward sign of their encounter in the elevator. Her long hair, formerly loose, was now smoothed back and clamped in place with a gold barrette. Its neatness only made him want to run his fingers through the silky length, feel its softness. Not the reaction she'd been aiming for, he was sure.

"Well?" she demanded. His silent appraisal was unnerving. "*Did* you cancel?"

"No." How beautiful her eyes were, he noted approvingly. They were a smoky blue, his favorite shade. "I told your father I'd be late but that I'd be there."

"Good." The predatory way Jake was eyeing her made Rebecca increasingly nervous. "Well, I know how much my father's looking forward to seeing you again after all this time, so I won't keep you. Goodbye, Mr. Fletcher."

He immediately corrected her. "Good night, maybe, but not goodbye. I'm sure we'll be running into each other again."

Not if I can help it, Rebecca thought to herself as she turned and walked away. She felt Jake's eyes on her as she hurried across the lobby to the main-floor ballroom where the banquet had been moved from its original location on the fourth floor.

Under the circumstances she couldn't help cursing fate. Of all the elevators in all the hotels in Washington, Jake had to walk into hers! She hadn't even known he was staying at this hotel. He didn't seem the type to enjoy the sedate old-world atmosphere evoked here. No doubt he thrived on danger and excitement.

As the banquet speakers droned on, Rebecca considered the likelihood that Jake might be practicing his interrogation techniques on her father. Not that it would take much to get her father to crack. He loved talking about her, especially to eligible bachelors. She groaned as she imagined the possibility—no, make that *probability*—of her father and Jake sharing a man-to-man talk about her.

As it turned out, Rebecca had good cause to be uneasy. Bill de Witt and Jake Fletcher were indeed discussing her. After eating every bit of Dorothy's delicious dinner, the two men had retired to Bill's study to enjoy a glass of brandy. As they had already discussed Bill's recent retirement and the state of the suspense novel as a genre, Jake decided it was time to bring up the woman who'd dominated his thoughts throughout dinner.

"I'm sorry your daughter wasn't able to join us," he said as he accepted the snifter of brandy Bill had poured for him.

"Rebecca's got a mind of her own," Bill replied with paternal resignation, but there was a gleam of humor in his blue eyes.

Remembering Rebecca's affronted huffiness, Jake murmured, "I got that impression."

"You did? When?"

Jake, who'd also been remembering the haunting smell of Rebecca's perfume and imagining the taste of her lips, needed a moment to recover. "What? Oh, I ran into your daughter at the hotel earlier this evening, and I have to say that she didn't look anything like a librarian."

Bill grinned. "Don't tell her that. She takes her profession very seriously. She takes everything very seriously."

Jake wondered if making love was one of the things Rebecca took seriously. Then he began wondering why she had been wearing that sexy black dress tonight. "Rebecca never did tell me what she was doing at the hotel," Jake casually noted.

"She's attending a Women in Careers dinner," Bill replied.

Jake was relieved to hear that she wasn't out on a date, although it seemed a shame to waste that dress on a crowd of women.

Unaware of his guest's thoughts, Bill continued speaking. "Rebecca's gotten involved with this career group ever since she moved back to Washington six months ago and began working at the Library of Congress. The cataloging position at the library was a godsend. She'd been having a tough time of it in Chicago, what with her husband's death and all."

Even though he'd been half expecting it, the news still shook Jake. He'd been hoping that his memory was mistaken, that Rebecca had never been married.

"Anyway," Bill went on, "after Ted died, Rebecca had to get a job to support herself and my granddaughter, Amy. Amy's almost four now, by the way."

So there was a child. A daughter. Jake was willing to bet that the little girl had Rebecca's beautiful smoky-blue eyes.

"Even though Rebecca got a job, her salary couldn't cover all the expenses, so she ended up selling the Chicago house and moving back here. I'm glad she did," Bill added. "Rebecca may be a grown woman of twenty-eight with a child of her own, but I still worry about her. With her and Amy living right upstairs, even if it is in a separate apartment, at least I can keep an eye on them."

Jake wanted to do more than just keep an eye on Rebecca. The strength of his feelings surprised him. It wasn't like him to be so interested in a woman with a ready-made family. Not that he disliked kids—after all he'd been one himself once—but he wasn't a man that would coo over babies. The truth was that he felt awkward around children.

"It's worked out wonderfully for all of us," Bill was saying. "This house is too big for one person, so I'm glad for the company. And it's convenient for Rebecca, too. She knows she can leave Amy with me or Dorothy when she goes to work. Of course, getting Rebecca to go out socially is something else again," he added in an aggrieved tone.

"Maybe she's still mourning the loss of her husband," Jake suggested. The idea of Rebecca carrying a torch for some other man made his stomach clench.

"I don't think that's the case," Bill replied, much to Jake's relief. "But getting information out of my daughter is harder than pulling hens' teeth." Bill shook his head in exasperation. "All I do know is that Ted was a real workaholic and very ambitious, blindly so. He was a futures commodities broker in the Chicago Stock Exchange. I also know that Rebecca would kill me if she found out I'd been discussing her private life like this."

"She does seem to have a temper," Jake recalled with amusement. She also had a lot of passion beneath that cool exterior, passion that he longed to explore.

"Under the circumstances, I think it would be better if we kept this conversation just between the two of us," Bill suggested. "That way we can avoid upsetting Rebecca."

Jake agreed. "Don't worry, my lips are sealed."

Rebecca was thinking about Jake's lips as she sat in the back of a taxicab headed for the Georgetown home she'd grown up in. Try as she might, she couldn't seem to forget that moment in the elevator when she thought he'd been about to kiss her. The incident had left her shaken. She had the uneasy feeling that Jake Fletcher was going to be a lot harder to ignore than her father's previous matchmaking candidates had been.

"Here we are, lady," the driver said. "That'll be $3.25."

Rebecca was so preoccupied that she handed him a five and told him to keep the change.

"Not very bright, Rebecca," she muttered to herself as she unlocked the front door. "You need the money more than that cabbie does."

Although their home was in a fairly prestigious Georgetown neighborhood, the de Witt family was not financially well off. Since her father's retirement, money had become tight. The house was tied up in an elaborate trust and couldn't be sold. Her father often referred to himself as a mere caretaker, struggling to keep up with the maintenance bills. But despite his grumbling, he loved the house, as did Rebecca and her older brother, Kent. After all, the stately brick house had been in the family for three generations. It was worth preserving.

As she stood in the front hallway, Rebecca experienced a familiar sense of homecoming. The Oriental throw rug beneath her feet was the same one she'd played on as a child. She used to pretend it was a magic carpet that would fly her out through the front door. And the Chippendale chair to her left still carried the mark where, at the advanced age of seven, she'd attempted to use a butter knife to carve her initials on one of the legs.

Even the air was filled with the familiar smells of home: the tanginess of lemon furniture polish, the lingering aroma of Dorothy's famous apple strudel and the rich scent of roses gathered from the tiny garden out back. No matter how bad things got in the world outside, inside this house Rebecca had always felt safe and protected. It was her refuge in the storm.

As the grandfather clock in the corner struck midnight, Rebecca noticed the thin stream of light coming from beneath the closed door to her father's study. She listened cautiously. Surely her father's guest must have left by now. But the telltale sound of masculine laughter told her that Jake was still there.

Her earlier feelings of warmth and security faded and were replaced with a restless uneasiness. She had the funny feeling that her father and Jake were up to something. Whatever it was, she didn't want to know about it. She'd had enough of Jake Fletcher and his whirlwind approach for one day.

Carefully, quietly, she tiptoed across the foyer and headed for the stairway leading to her own apartment upstairs. She'd made it up only two stairs when a creaky plank gave her away. The door to the study opened, spilling light into the hall and spotlighting her as she stood poised for flight.

"Ah, there you are," her father announced happily. "I thought I heard you come in."

Reluctantly Rebecca turned to face her father. When she saw Jake standing beside him, smiling confidently, she immediately became suspicious.

"Wonderful news, my dear," Bill went on to say. "Jake's going to be staying with us while he's here in Washington."

Over my dead body, Rebecca silently vowed.

Two

"Father, I'd like to speak to you in private," Rebecca declared. "Now please," she added with meaningful emphasis.

"Not now, dear. We've got company," Bill objected mildly.

"That's all right, Bill," Jake drawled. "Don't worry about me. Just pretend I'm part of the family."

That'll be the day. Rebecca's inhospitable thoughts were clearly voiced in the disapproving look she gave Jake.

So you don't want me to stay. What are you going to do about it? Jake silently challenged her.

Bill looked as though he approved of the visual interplay between Rebecca and Jake. He might have plans for his daughter, but he would have a hard time convincing Rebecca of their merit. "Is what you have to say so important that it can't wait until morning?" Bill asked.

Rebecca stuck to her guns. "Yes, it is that important. And no, it can't wait."

"All right," Bill reluctantly agreed. "Excuse us a moment, Jake. Go on back into the study and make yourself comfortable. Feel free to pour yourself another brandy. This shouldn't take long."

"I wouldn't be too sure about that, Bill," Jake murmured. "Your daughter looks pretty upset to me. I don't think she's going to let you off easy this time."

Bill chuckled.

Rebecca was not similarly amused, a fact she communicated with a stony glare.

"Watch out—you don't want your contact lens falling out again," Jake warned her mockingly.

"We'll talk upstairs, Father," Rebecca stated. Taking hold of her father's arm, she almost dragged him up the stairs.

After storming through the double doors leading to her apartment, Rebecca was all set to read her father the riot act. Unfortunately, the housekeeper's presence thwarted her plans.

Dorothy often had a deterring effect on outbursts of temper. One look from her steely, pale blue eyes was enough to make a grown man quake in his boots. But even though she had the outward demeanor of a marine drill sergeant, inside she was a warm and loving mother hen with a real soft spot for children. From the first day she'd been in the de Witt household, Dorothy had gently but firmly run the family that was trying so hard to keep itself together in the face of Mrs. de Witt's incurable cancer. She had taken twelve-year-old Rebecca under her wing, and to this day treated her as if she were one of her own. That meant babysitting for Rebecca's daughter, Amy, when the occasion called for it, and it also meant speaking her mind whether the occasion called for it or not.

"I thought you still had company," Dorothy said now with a disapproving look in their direction. "What are you two doing up here?"

"That's what I'd like to know." Bill passed the disapproval on to Rebecca.

"I needed to talk to Dad in private," Rebecca stated defensively.

Dorothy got huffy, a specialty of hers. "Well, make it quick. It's rude to leave company alone. And be quiet about it, or you'll wake up Amy. I'll go see if your guest wants anything before I leave. He must think you two are nuts, coming up here like this and leaving him down there all by himself." Muttering about manners, Dorothy marched downstairs.

Frustrated at having to speak softly when she wanted to yell, Rebecca quietly exclaimed, "Father, how could you!"

"How could I what?" Bill played innocent. "You're the one who upset Dorothy, not me."   "I'm not talking about Dorothy. I'm talking about Jake Fletcher. How could you invite that man to stay here?"

"Very easily," her father answered. "He's a friend of mine."

Rebecca's "Hah!" was patently disbelieving. "This is just another one of your matchmaking ploys. Well, you've gone too far this time."

Bill shook his head at his daughter's agitation. "Rebecca, my dear, you're getting paranoid. Actually, several years ago I extended Jake an open invitation to stay with me if he should ever return to Washington. Since that invitation was made before you even moved in with me, I don't see how you can accuse me of matchmaking."

"I can accuse you because I know how you think. You think that Amy should have a father, and you've been doing everything in your power to try to hook me up with a man. Every time I turn around you're dangling another supposedly eligible bachelor in front of my nose. I haven't complained before—I know you're only trying to be helpful—but inviting Jake Fletcher to stay here is not helpful, it's impossible."

"Nothing is impossible, Rebecca. Surely I've told you that often enough."

"This is."

"I don't understand why you're getting so upset about this," Bill mused with a shake of his head. "You'll be at work all day, so you'll hardly even notice that Jake is staying here. Besides, it'll be nice for me to have another man around the house. I'm outnumbered three to one as it is now, with you, Dorothy and Amy."

His comment hurt her feelings. "Dorothy doesn't live in, and you invited Amy and me to stay here with you. I didn't realize we were such an inconvenience."

"You're not an inconvenience." Her father's look was reproachful. "You know I love having you and Amy with me. But that doesn't mean I wouldn't like to have conversation with a man now and again."

She knew her father was deliberately playing on her emotions, but she also knew that there was a great deal of truth in what he said. He respected Jake and no doubt would enjoy having him as a houseguest. And it was his house, after all. Nonetheless, her surrender was reluctant. "How long would he be staying?"

"Only until he finishes the research for his next book."

"How long will that be?"

"Not very long." Bill smiled reassuringly. "Now, I really must get back downstairs. As Dorothy so eloquently pointed out, Jake will think me terribly rude for having deserted him like this."

"I doubt that manners are a high-priority item for Jake Fletcher," she commented tartly.

"But they are a priority for me." Bill gave her a worried frown. "You will be nice to him, won't you? Polite? Hospitable?"

Rebecca wasn't about to surrender that much. "I won't shoot him, even though I may be tempted" was all she promised.

"You two appear to have gotten off on the wrong foot. Care to tell me about it?"

"Didn't Jake fill you in already?"

Bill shook his head. "All he said was that he'd met you at the hotel on the way over here."

Rebecca had no intention of relating the exact details of their meeting. The episode in the elevator was one she wanted to forget. "It's a long story, and you've got a guest waiting for you downstairs," she reminded him.

"That's right. The plan is for Jake to check out of the hotel and move into the spare bedroom downstairs tomorrow," Bill said.

"That's just dandy," she muttered. "Let's hope he's a fast researcher."

There was a twinkle in Bill's eye as he acknowledged, "Jake does have a reputation for being a fast worker."

Rebecca already knew Jake was a fast worker. Look how quickly he'd moved into her father's house—and her life. She didn't like it. And she didn't like the way she wasn't able to sleep that night for worrying about it.

Rebecca received another disturbing surprise the next day while at work. Immersed in her cataloging, she suddenly got the uneasy feeling that someone was staring at her. Looking up, she found Jake standing there.

Jake's first thought was that Rebecca looked more like a librarian than she had last night. For one thing, she was wearing tortoiseshell glasses. Her cream-colored blouse had every button buttoned, and her hair was held away from her face with a pair of tortoiseshell combs. To some she might have appeared straitlaced, but Jake knew better. He suddenly had the strongest urge to kiss her.

Rebecca realized that she looked different than she had last night, but that was no reason for Jake to stare at her. So she was wearing glasses. So what? Her reason for wearing them was very practical; she preferred them to her contacts because of the dust. A lot of the books had gained several layers of dust by the time they made it to her desk—the same desk that Jake had just casually perched upon.

Irritated by his presumption, she said, "Whatever it is, the answer is no. And get off my desk. You're squishing that book."

They both reached for the book at the same time. Their hands touched. The contact, slight though it was, rattled her. When he deliberately brushed his thumb across the back of her fingers, she yanked her hand away and said, "Would you please quit fooling around?"

"Me? Fool around? Right here?" Jake looked about, arching one eyebrow. "In the middle of the Library of Congress?"

Rebecca wished she had the luxury of an office so she could confront Jake in private. As it was, she was very much aware of the other catalogers in the room with her. They were all viewing Jake with interest. Her only hope was to get rid of him as quickly as possible, before he caused any more trouble. "Why are you here?"

"I came to see you," he answered.

"Then you made a wasted trip."

"That's not what your father said."

As he'd intended, Jake's comment grabbed her attention. "What did my father say?"

"That you were the person I should contact to help me with my research."

"I'm not a research librarian. I'm a cataloging librarian," she told him.

"I know that. But I figured you could give me some pointers."

"I doubt that. Besides, you don't seem to be the kind of man who needs or accepts pointers."

"Really? What kind of man do I seem to be to you?"

Belatedly, Rebecca saw the folly in pursuing this subject. "I don't know you well enough to answer that question."

"We can rectify that."

"I don't want to," she retorted.

He shook his head at her. "You know, if I didn't know better, I never would have guessed that beneath that frosty exterior you put on, there beats the heart of a passionate woman." Leaning closer, he murmured, "But I do know better, so your attempts to give me frostbite aren't going to work."

She glared at him. "If I wanted to give you anything, Mr. Fletcher, it would be a black eye! You took advantage of my situation in that elevator last night."

"Sweetheart, this is much too public a place for us to discuss what we shared last night," Jake said, loudly enough for everyone in the immediate vicinity to overhear him.

With all eyes on her, Rebecca felt compelled to make a hurried explanation to her co-workers. "It's not the way it sounds."

"No, it was better than that," Jake inserted.

"It was not!" she denied.

"It was for me. It wasn't good for you, too?"

"It was extremely forgettable," she shot back before realizing that, by doing so, she only fueled the fire.

"Then I guess it's a good thing I've moved in with you. I look forward to reawakening your memory, among other things."

"He hasn't moved in with me. He's moved in with my father," she explained to the room at large. Everyone had stopped working anyway, and they were all eavesdropping with varying degrees of discretion. "In case you're wondering, this man is Jake Fletcher, the suspense writer. Some of you may have read his last book, *Vengeance*, and remembered the stereotyped librarian in it. Attila the Hun had more charm than that librarian."

Murmurs of professional indignation emanated from those who'd read the book or heard about it.

"I've seen the error of my ways," Jake declared dramatically. "I'm here to make amends."

"You're here to make trouble," Rebecca muttered under her breath. "And you're succeeding." She was forced to abandon her position behind her desk in favor of finding a little privacy. "We'll finish this discussion out in the hallway."

"It was nice almost meeting all of you," Jake drawled to the roomful of librarians.

"You've got no right coming in here and making a scene," Rebecca fumed once they were both safely in the hallway. Too angry to stand still, she was pacing back and forth. "I've only been working here a few months, and this little stunt of yours could get me into trouble. So please do me a big favor and stay away from me."

"That may be hard to do, considering the fact that I'm living in the same house with you."

"The fact that you're my father's temporary houseguest doesn't give you the right to interrupt my work here at the library."

"I'm here to do research."

"If you need assistance with your research, I suggest you contact someone in the reference division."

"My research needs are somewhat unusual. I'm not sure someone in the reference division would be able to handle them."

"Your needs are *your* problem," she retorted.

"What about your needs?"

"What about them?"

"Are they being satisfied?"

Fire flashed in her eyes. She was suddenly so angry that she was shaking. He had no right taunting her this way. Not trusting herself to speak, she swung around and marched off. She'd only taken a few steps when his hand on her arm stopped her.

"I'm sorry," he said quietly. "I was out of line."

His apology was the last thing she'd expected to hear. She looked at him distrustfully and wondered what he was up to now.

"Look, we seem to have gotten off on the wrong foot here. I dropped by because I wanted to clear up the misunderstanding from yesterday."

"Which misunderstanding?" she asked warily.

"About my dinner invitation last night. If you'll think back, I never actually pinned down the invitation to any specific time or date. You're the one who assumed I was ready to dump your father and go out with you instead."

Rebecca remained silent as she realized what he said was true.

Looking at her with challenging directness, Jake stated, "I want you to know that I like and respect your father. I wouldn't do anything to hurt him."

Rebecca got the impression that Jake didn't respect many people, but that really wasn't any of her concern. So long as her father wasn't hurt, she could take care of herself, and she planned on doing so by staying out of Jake's way.

"It won't go away, you know," he said, as if reading her thoughts.

"What won't?"

"This attraction between us."

"I don't know what you're talking about."

Placing his hand in the center of her back, Jake gently tugged her into his arms. "I'm talking about this," he murmured before kissing her.

His lips were warm, and his approach was skillful. He knew exactly what he was doing, Rebecca dimly realized. His lips moved over hers in a provocative play that bordered on intimacy but refrained from intimidation. He was inviting her to kiss him back, tempting her, tantalizing her.

The effect was electrifying. Logical thought temporarily evaporated, leaving her vulnerable. By the time Rebecca found the strength to struggle, the damage had already been done. For one brief moment she'd responded to him, answering his declaration of desire with one of her own. Aghast at what she'd revealed, she hurriedly freed herself from his embrace. His lips left hers with the greatest of reluctance.

Rebecca took two giant steps backward and lifted trembling fingers to her mouth. The wild impact of his kiss had left her dizzy from the force of her emotions. Drawing in an unsteady breath, she gave Jake a how-could-you look.

Jake returned her gaze with a frustrated look of his own. Just when he thought he was getting to her, she retreated. That kiss they'd just shared had only increased his hunger for her. But it had also proved that this attraction was not one-sided. Like it or not, she did want him.

That realization made Jake smile. He didn't say a word; he didn't have to. The message he sent was received loud and clear. *I get to you.* Aloud he said, "I'll see you later." He made it sound like an intimate promise.

He was gone before Rebecca had the time to collect her scattered thoughts. There was no point in denying it, at least not to herself. Jake did get to her. That kiss they'd just shared had practically steamed up her glasses. The question was, what was she going to do about it?

So far her defenses weren't proving to be very effective. Sure, afterward she was able to feel indignation and anger, but while Jake was kissing her, all she'd felt was excitement and pleasure. And therein lay the danger.

She had no doubt that she was merely a passing challenge to Jake. The thrill of the chase would appeal to a predator like him. He was obviously anticipating sweeping her off her feet and hustling her into his bed. She recognized the signs. Her husband, Ted, had swept her off her feet, declared it was love at first sight and kissed away her reservations. They'd been married within the month. It had all seemed so romantic.

Looking back now, she knew that Ted had been motivated not by passion but by practicality. He hadn't had time to waste looking for a wife. The Chicago brokerage firm where he'd wanted to work had an unwritten policy of preferring the stability of a married man. Ted had been scheduled for an interview, and time had been running out. He'd ended up taking Rebecca to Chicago on their honeymoon. The interview was successful, and Ted had gotten the job.

Despite the evidence to the contrary, Rebecca had remained romantically optimistic. At twenty-three she'd been blindly in love. Perhaps her definition of love was different from Ted's, but she knew they could work it out. Reality had hit a few months later when she discovered she was pregnant. She and Ted had never discussed children; Ted was rarely home long enough to discuss anything. But she'd been certain that he'd be as excited as she was with the news.

He hadn't been. Ted had coldly informed her that he wasn't sure he ever wanted to be a father. There were other things he'd rather do with his time and money. Rebecca's final hope was that once the baby was born, he'd change his mind. She should have known better.

Ted hadn't seen any beauty in his baby daughter's face. He had no interest in Amy's first step or her first tooth. He had no interest in Amy, period. The commodities future market was his only concern. When Amy was eighteen months old, Ted abruptly left the brokerage firm, cashed in all their savings and used the money to form his own investment firm. He invested heavily in several speculative deals that hadn't panned out. In fact he'd been literally wheeling and dealing, driving while negotiating a new get-rich-quick scheme on his car phone, when he'd run a red light. The ensuing collision had killed him and seriously injured the other driver.

That was two years ago. Gradually Rebecca had gotten over the shock, the guilt, the anger. And she'd learned one very important lesson. Life was short, and to make it sweet you had to know what you wanted.

Rebecca did know what she wanted. She wanted a man who had his priorities straight. A man who put family at the top of his list, not at the bottom. A man who had staying power.

Equally important, Rebecca knew what she didn't want. She didn't want to be swept off her feet again. Jake was only amusing himself at her expense; he was going to be in town only a week or two. Now that she knew how he operated, she'd have to ensure that he didn't sneak up on her again.

As for the present, she couldn't put off returning to her desk any longer. She wasn't bombarded with questions when she walked into the cataloging office, but then, she hadn't really been expecting that. The other librarians were too professional to be so obvious. Instead, the inquiries came one by one throughout the remainder of the afternoon.

The first comment came from the cataloger at the next desk, Nancy Simon. Of all the people she worked with,

Nancy was the closest to Rebecca's age. While not close friends, the two women had a good working relationship. "You never mentioned that Jake Fletcher was a friend of yours."

Rebecca immediately corrected her. "He's not a friend of mine. He's a friend of my father's."

"I wish he were a friend of *my* father's," Nancy murmured wistfully.

The second observation came from Marian Jacobs, one of the senior catalogers, and was sandwiched in between a consultation about a book's classification. "I must say that Jake Fletcher looks different in real life than he does in those photos on the back cover of his books. He looks dangerous."

Without thinking, Rebecca said, "He is dangerous. The man would try the patience of a nun."

Having overheard Rebecca's comment, Nancy added her two cents' worth. "I think he'd also catch the attention of a nun."

Marian stunned Rebecca by admitting, "He certainly caught my attention, and I'm a grandmother!"

Marian and Nancy shared a laugh.

Rebecca couldn't believe what she was hearing. This kind of lighthearted banter might have been characteristic of Nancy, but Marian Jacobs? While polite, the older, more experienced librarians like Marian had always kept their distance from Rebecca, who after six months at the Library of Congress was still considered the new kid on the block.

"Is something wrong, Rebecca?" Marian asked. "You look surprised."

"I . . . it's just that we don't usually discuss such personal issues," Rebecca replied, at a loss to explain this sudden character shift.

"Maybe we should," Marian stated with a wink and a smile.

There was no doubt about it, Rebecca decided. Jake Fletcher should be labeled Hazardous. If he had this effect on the normally ultrareserved Marian, anything was possible!

That evening when Rebecca got home her first order of business was confronting her father. He was hiding out in his study, but she tracked him down.

"Where's your houseguest?" she demanded, wanting to make sure the coast was clear before she launched into her attack.

"I'm not sure," her father replied, "but he isn't in the house, if that's what you're asking."

"Fine. We need to set up some ground rules here."

"Rules? For what?"

"For you and your houseguest. At the top of the list: no matchmaking!"

Bill deliberately misunderstood her. "Jake has been matchmaking?"

"Jake has been making trouble, at your instigation. He showed up at the cataloging department today and disrupted everyone's work." She was tempted to add that Jake had kissed her but decided that, knowing her father, the information would only spur him on. "Jake said that you'd sent him."

"I didn't send him, exactly."

"Then what did you do, exactly?"

"Has she read you your rights yet, Bill?" Jake inquired from his position near the door.

He'd done it again, Rebecca thought to herself with a frown. Snuck up on her, caught her unaware. She turned to glance at him and concluded that he looked too dangerous for her peace of mind. His dark slacks and shirt only added to his aura of dynamic masculinity.

She didn't understand his reference to rights, however. "What are you talking about?"

"It sounds to me as if I walked into the middle of an interrogation," he replied.

"What you walked into is the middle of a private discussion."

"Nonsense," Bill denied. "Don't let my daughter make you feel unwelcome, Jake."

"Rebecca makes me feel a lot of things, but unwelcome isn't one of them." Jake's voice was full of hidden meaning.

Bill hastily intervened before Rebecca could say anything. "How did your research go, Jake? Did you find what you were looking for?"

Jake didn't take his eyes off of Rebecca. "I found more than I expected," he replied in a disturbingly soft voice.

He's just trying to sweet-talk you, she warned herself before issuing a warning to Jake. "It sounds to me as if this time you've bitten off more than you can chew."

"I haven't really had a chance to sink my teeth into this project yet, but when I do, you'll be the first to know," he assured her.

It took an effort of will for Rebecca to pull her eyes away from his. "Don't bother," she muttered.

"Oh, it's no bother. It'll be my pleasure."

Thinking about pleasure made her realize how long it had been since she'd experienced it. Oh, not the pleasure of a sunset or a beautiful day—she'd felt that often enough. But Jake hadn't been referring to that kind of pleasure, and she knew it. He'd been talking about the pleasure that comes when a man and a woman make love together, sharing the deepest intimacies.

Rebecca's breath caught, and her heart beat faster. He'd done it again. Gotten to her. And this time he'd done it from halfway across the room, with her own father looking on! Dismayed, she retreated to the relative safety of the kitchen and the calming company of her daughter, Amy.

"Mommy!" Amy rushed forward to wrap her arms around Rebecca's knees. "I was very, very, very good today."

Looking down into Amy's smiling face, Rebecca returned the smile and nudged the glasses her daughter wore higher onto her tiny nose. Amy was such a little thing, the glasses were almost bigger than she was. But wearing them was the only way to correct the vision disorder the little girl had developed.

Rebecca had worried that wearing the glasses might worsen Amy's already intense shyness, but the child behaviorist she'd consulted didn't think that was the case. Amy's shyness was a way for her to cope with all the changes she'd had in her young life: Ted's death, Rebecca's return to the workplace, their move from Chicago. It was a lot for a small child to cope with. It was even a lot for Rebecca to cope with at times.

Amy's tugging on Rebecca's skirt returned her thoughts to the present. "Mommy, look!"

"What a beautiful picture!" Rebecca exclaimed. "Did you draw that all by yourself?"

Amy nodded proudly. "Dotty watched me." Amy was the only one allowed to use the abbreviation of Dorothy's name. "And I helped her cook. I putted the carrots in the bowl."

"I put the carrots in the bowl," Rebecca corrected her.

"No, you didn't, Mommy. You were working. I putted the carrots in the bowl all by myself. Dotty watched. She hurted herself with a knife and said a bad word, that's how come I got to help her cook. I said she could use one of my

Smurf Band-Aids to make it better. That's sharing, right, Mommy?"

"Right, pumpkin. How about sharing a hug with me?"

Scooping her daughter up into her arms, Rebecca gladly accepted Amy's hug. Coming home to the unconditional acceptance of a child usually put everything else into perspective. Today, unfortunately, the treatment wasn't working as well as it should. Rebecca knew who was to blame for that; he was in the study with her father right now.

Sighing, she sat down on a kitchen chair and settled Amy on her lap. "Did Grandpa tell you he's got company?"

Amy nodded again and frowned. "Is that man gonna stay?" the little girl asked in a whisper.

"For a few days."

Amy didn't look happy to hear the news. Rebecca knew how she felt. "Could you do me a favor, Amy? Would you draw me another picture to match this one?"

The little girl nodded, slipped off her lap and headed for the scaled-down worktable in the alcove near the window. The son of one of Rebecca's father's friends had made the desk. Rebecca recalled ruefully that the recently divorced carpenter had been another example of her father's match-making attempts.

"You look flustered," Dorothy noted as she bustled around the kitchen. "Something wrong?"

"Can't you speak to him, Dorothy? Tell him that match-making went out with the horse and buggy?"

"I presume you're talking about your father."

"And his guest. The two of them are probably in the study right now," Rebecca muttered, "concocting some new scheme."

"I doubt that."

"You don't know Jake Fletcher."

"Neither do you," Dorothy pointed out. "But your father does."

"Not really. Father sees Jake through rose-colored glasses as the star pupil who made good."

Dorothy added some salt to the boiling pot of carrots before fixing Rebecca with a direct stare. "And how do you see Jake?"

"I'd rather not see him at all," Rebecca retorted. "So Amy and I will be eating upstairs tonight."

Hearing her name, Amy looked up from the drawing she was working on. "Can we have sausages and cookies?"

"We can have something even better, sausages and baby trees." The term had a much better success rate than the vegetable's proper name of broccoli.

"Oh, goody!" Amy exclaimed. "I love baby trees. Someday I'm gonna grow up into a tree."

Rebecca shared a smile with Dorothy. "I'm sure her career goals will change as she gets older."

After the dinner Rebecca had cooked in their own compact kitchen upstairs, she gave Amy a bath and then read her a story aptly titled, *Terry the Tree*. But once her daughter dropped off to sleep, Rebecca became restless.

Deciding that she might as well put her energy to some use, she looked for the tote bag she carried to and from work. There were several issues of professional journals and cataloging policy statements that she was behind in reading. Unfortunately she couldn't find any sign of the tote bag. Then she remembered she'd left it in her father's study when she'd confronted him earlier.

If she went downstairs to retrieve it, there was always the chance that she'd run into Jake. Still, it was only nine-thirty, so her father would be with him. Fed up with hiding, Rebecca left her apartment and went downstairs. Since the door to her father's study was open, she walked right in, intending to grab her tote bag and leave. To her dismay, Jake was there alone.

She saw the challenging gleam in his eyes and refused to give him the satisfaction of seeing her run away.

Spotting the notebook on his lap she said, "I see you're keeping busy."

"That's right." He indicated her jeans and sweatshirt with an approving nod. "And I see you've discarded your librarian's disguise."

"It's not a disguise," she denied.

"No? What would you call those glasses you were wearing earlier today?"

"I call them practical. I wear my glasses whenever I'm cataloging a backlog of dusty old books."

"Sure. Whatever you say."

"You don't believe me?"

He gave her a look of pseudo-innocence. "I didn't say that."

"You didn't have to," she muttered. "You have a habit of saying one thing and meaning another."

"I'm not the only one."

She decided to ignore his last comment. "Where's my father?"

Jake gave her that slow smile she was coming to recognize, and even worse, appreciate. She knew he only used it when he felt he was getting to her. It was his way of acknowledging her change of subject and telling her he'd let her get away with it, this time. "Bill drove Dorothy home. It's pouring outside."

Rebecca walked over to the window and held the sheer curtain aside. She'd always liked the rain. Her father's car, on the other hand, had always had an aversion to dampness. "I'm surprised the car started," she noted conversationally. "It's a tiny Triumph Spitfire and can be quite temperamental. Dad doesn't take it out very often. Competition for parking space is pretty fierce around here.''

Jake surprised her by saying, ''I know what you mean. When I lived in D.C. I had a Camaro. Great car, but there wasn't anyplace to park it. I ended up selling it.''

Rebecca omitted telling him that she, too, had once had a Camaro. She'd loved that car, but she'd had to sell it before leaving Chicago. She'd needed the money. Blocking out those memories, she continued their conversation. ''How long did you live here?''

''Six years.'' His voice hardened. ''Six long years.''

''It sounds as if you couldn't wait to get away.''

''I couldn't.''

She turned to face him. ''Then why did you come back?''

For an instant his eyes were shadowy. ''To exorcise old ghosts.'' He paused a moment, as if lost in thought. When he spoke again his voice was deliberately lighter. ''And to research my next book. I was working on the story line when you walked in.''

''I'll let you get on with it, then. I don't want to disturb you.''

''Too late. You've been disturbing me ever since I saw you in that elevator.''

''I'm sure you'll get over it,'' she retorted. Jake was looking at her with that familiar gleam in his eyes. She decided that it must have been some trick of the lighting that had made him look so serious a few moments ago. He was certainly back to his old audacious self now. ''If you'll excuse me, I've got to get back upstairs.''

''Going back into hiding, huh?''

''I have not been hiding. I've been spending time with my daughter.''

"So, when do I get to meet this daughter of yours?" Jake asked.

Rebecca answered with unmistakable finality. "You don't."

Three

Rebecca's words turned Jake into a cold remote stranger. She could see the change come over him. It was as if a switch had been turned off. His teasing warmth vanished and in its place was that dark side she'd sensed the first time he'd ever spoken to her. Rebecca shivered—even having Jake drive her crazy with suggestive remarks was preferable to this.

"My daughter is very shy of strangers," Rebecca explained, albeit belatedly.

The excuse sounded lame to Jake. He had a strong suspicion that Rebecca didn't want him to meet Amy because she didn't want him intruding any further on her little family circle. It shouldn't have upset him. Jake was accustomed to being on the outside and it had never bothered him before. Hell, he'd spent most of his life feeling removed from it all—the pain and the joy.

In the past, that was the way he'd wanted it. He'd come to accept the fact that he was a loner. He'd not only welcomed the distance, he'd insisted on it. But the decision to stay isolated had always been his. He didn't like the idea of someone else locking him out. He didn't like it at all.

Why was she so adamant about not wanting him to meet her kid? Could it be that she didn't think he was good enough? After all, their backgrounds were worlds apart. Rebecca had been raised in this fancy house in Georgetown, a house with a heritage. The only heritage he had wasn't even worth remembering.

"So you don't want me meeting your daughter because she's shy, is that it?" He spoke each word with slow deliberation.

Rebecca nodded.

"I don't buy that. What's really brought on all this maternal protectiveness?"

Rebecca's earlier regret at upsetting Jake was fading fast. He had no right jumping down her throat. What was this, the third degree? He was making her feel as if she'd committed some terrible criminal act. "I already told you but if you don't believe me, that's your problem. I don't understand what you're getting so upset about anyway."

"You tell me that I'm not fit to even *meet* your daughter and you don't understand why I'm upset?"

"I never said you weren't fit," she denied.

"You may not have said it, but you were sure thinking it."

"How do you know what I'm thinking? What are you, a mind reader?"

"It doesn't take a mind reader to see that you've cast me in the role of the Big Bad Wolf."

"And who's fault is that?" she shot back. "You've been acting like a wolf ever since I met you."

"And that's why you don't want me to meet your daughter?"

"No, that's not why!" Rebecca's voice rose angrily. "I told you, Amy is frightened of strangers. Since you're only going to be here a few days, I think it would be best if she weren't pushed into meeting you."

Jake immediately latched on to the last part of her statement. "And what makes you think I'll be here only a few days?"

"My father said that you'd be staying only until your research was finished," Rebecca replied confidently.

"Ah, but that was before I met his beautiful if incredibly stubborn daughter."

"Don't make the mistake of changing your plans on my account," she told him. "You'll be wasting your time."

"I don't think so."

"I don't care what you think, just leave my daughter alone. And leave me alone."

"That's it," he taunted as she marched toward the open study door. "Go ahead and walk out in the middle of a fight."

She turned to confront him. "Fighting is more up your alley than it is mine. You may find it amusing; I don't."

Jake reached around her to close the study door. "I can think of a lot of other things I'd find more amusing."

"I'm sure you can, but I'm not interested in any of them."

"You're interested in *me*." He said the words matter-of-factly, while looking at her in a way that was anything but.

"How many times do I have to tell you? There's nothing between you and me! I met you two days ago, and you haven't exactly gone out of your way to endear yourself to me since then," she added with a glare.

Jake nodded understandingly. "You're angry because I kissed you today."

"Yes."

"And you liked it," he added, "which makes you even madder."

"What is this, a psychology lesson?"

Jake shrugged. "I'm just explaining the situation to you, in case you're having trouble figuring it out."

"The only trouble I'm having is with you," she snapped.

"Really?" Bracing a hand on either side of her head, Jake leaned closer. "That's funny because the only trouble *I'm* having is with *you*."

"I haven't done anything."

"That's true. Aside from returning my kiss, you haven't done anything. That's the problem. You tell me one thing, but your kiss told me something else. You can see how I'd be confused."

Rebecca couldn't see anything. She'd made the mistake of closing her eyes to avoid looking at him.

"Open your eyes," he ordered softly. "I want you to see what you do to me."

Her eyes flew open, and she glared at him. "I wish you'd stop ordering me around," she said in what she hoped was a cool voice.

"I wish you'd stop talking and kiss me," he replied in a warm whisper.

Without breaking their eye contact, he lowered his head until his lips touched hers with unhurried care. The warm exploration was slow and sensuous as he once again began coaxing her into responding. It was as if they were picking up where their kiss this afternoon had left off. Only this time she wasn't wearing her glasses, so there were no barriers.

Rebecca tried keeping her eyes open, but it didn't help. Not when he was sampling her as if she were an exquisite delicacy to be savored, brushing his mouth across hers; always moving, always tempting, but never satisfying. Unable to resist, she finally parted her lips and invited him to deepen the kiss. Her response fired his passion.

She forgot all the reasons why she shouldn't be doing this. Who could think coherently while being kissed so demandingly? She certainly couldn't; she didn't even want to try.

She wanted this pleasure to go on. So she moved the hands she'd been using to hold Jake off and slid them around his waist to his back. Muttering his approval, Jake pulled her to him. His hands were entwined in her long silky hair as he shifted the angle of their lips.

Trembling with excitement, Rebecca began making moves of her own. She ran the tip of her tongue across his lower lip, tasting him, teasing him. She pressed the palms of her hands against his back. He was so strong, so warm to the touch.

Jake was delighted with her newfound boldness and responded by sliding his hands beneath her sweatshirt. Rebecca felt as if she were on fire. The touch of his devilish fingers on her bare skin had her burning inside. His hand was hovering over the tempting curve of her breast when a little girl's scream shattered the silence.

"Mommy!"

Rebecca gasped and broke free. "Amy! She must be having a nightmare." Tugging the study door open, Rebecca ran upstairs leaving a frustrated Jake behind.

Upon reaching Amy's room, Rebecca turned on the light before hurrying to her daughter's bedside. "It's all right, honey. Mommy's right here. What's wrong?"

"M...m...m-monsters," the little girl gasped in fright before diving into her mother's arms.

"No, there are no monsters here." Rebecca ran a soothing hand over Amy's back. Amy had been having these nightmares about monsters for some time now; she'd begun having them back in Chicago. "Look, the light's on now. It was just a bad dream. Look around the room." She coaxed the little girl's face away from her shoulder. "See? It's okay. There aren't any monsters."

"Th...th-they hide!"

"No, they don't. Monsters aren't real. They were just part of your bad dreams. But you're awake now. And I'm here."

"Stay with me," Amy begged.

Rebecca did. Amy slept peacefully for the rest of the night, but Rebecca had plenty of disturbing dreams. All of them involved Jake and the completion of what they'd started in the study. In one version she slapped his face and marched away from him, but in another they sank to the floor and made love.

It didn't take a psychiatrist to figure out that the contradictory scenarios reflected her conflicting emotions. As Rebecca prepared Amy's breakfast the next morning, she continued to brood about her reaction to Jake's kiss last night. There hadn't been any ambivalence then, she'd responded wholeheartedly. But her heart wouldn't stay whole very long if she got involved with Jake.

"You look sad, Mommy," Amy noted. "Wanna hug?" She held out her arms.

Rebecca gathered her close and gave her such a huge hug that Amy squealed. "That tickles!"

"Thanks, pumpkin. I needed that."

If only all of my needs were so easy to fulfill, Rebecca thought wistfully.

Rebecca was relieved to make it out of the house without running into Jake. But when she arrived at work she was discouraged to find that the cataloging office was still buzzing from Jake's visit yesterday. Consequently, she didn't get a lot of work done.

After a late lunch Rebecca returned to her desk to find an unfamiliar folder on her desk.

"What's this?" she asked with a curious glance in Nancy's direction.

"They heard over in the fiction section that you knew Jake Fletcher so they sent over a folder of clippings on him. His life sounds as mysterious as something out of one of his novels," Nancy said. "You really should read it."

Rebecca didn't want to read it; she knew she shouldn't. She was already far too interested in Jake Fletcher as it was.

But the folder held the tempting possibility of finding out what made him tick. Maybe if she knew more about him, she'd be able to handle him better.

Handle might not be the appropriate word to use, she decided as memories of last night returned. Hoping to exorcise the disturbing images of her hands on his body, Rebecca put off opening the folder until the end of the day. By then she was sure she'd regained enough perspective that she'd be able to read the material objectively.

It wasn't that easy. The first article she read was from a popular Washington glossy magazine and included a large color photograph of Jake that dramatized his dark side. There was a James Dean gleam of rebellion in his eyes. Jake wasn't smiling, and he stared directly into the camera, as if warning the cameraman he wouldn't tolerate having another picture taken. He was wearing a black suit jacket with a white shirt, the top button of which was undone. His tie was loosened and slightly askew.

The accompanying article had been written after Jake's first book was published. The writer made a few references to Jake's mysterious past and his police training. As far as practical information went, there was very little of it. Aside from a brief comment about his growing up on the tough streets of Detroit, nothing was written about Jake's life before he joined the police force.

His more recent history was just as hazy. Jake Fletcher was his real name. He didn't seem to have a permanent address; no family, no roots, no responsibilities. Now she knew why her father had always written Jake in care of his publisher.

Jake's popularity with women was obvious—she noticed several pictures of him in the company of gorgeous model-types. The comment was made that he was rarely seen with the same woman twice. He'd never been married.

Rebecca didn't learn much she hadn't already known or suspected, but somehow seeing it there in black and white made it all the more concrete. She and Jake had nothing in common. So his kisses were fantastic and being in his arms almost irresistible. She wasn't the first woman to find him attractive and she wouldn't be the last.

Rebecca had gone this route before—had let her feelings for Ted control her judgment and her life. She'd stuck her head in the sand and ignored their intrinsic differences. She wouldn't make that same mistake twice. She wanted a family man, something Jake showed no signs of becoming.

When Jake first entered Bill's study he thought it was empty, but then he saw a pair of legs swinging from Bill's red leather wing chair. Judging from the frilly pink socks and Minnie Mouse gym shoes, the legs belonged to a little girl. Jake smiled, pleased by the prospect of finally being able to meet Rebecca's daughter.

He moved closer, hoping to catch a glimpse of Amy before she saw him. His plan backfired. She saw him the same instant he saw her.

She wasn't at all what he'd expected. This little girl didn't look anything like Rebecca; she wasn't even cute. Her hair was a nondescript sort of brown and she wore a pair of thick glasses that covered most of her face.

"Amy?"

She was up and out of the chair in a flash. Her pigtails flew behind her as she raced for the door, where she rammed into Bill.

"Hey, what's this, poppet?" Bill asked. "Where are you off to in such a big hurry?"

Amy hid behind her grandfather's leg.

"I'm afraid it's my fault, Bill," Jake answered on Amy's behalf. "I surprised her."

Bill leaned down to pick up his granddaughter. She immediately twined her thin arms in a stranglehold around his neck and hid her face in his shoulder. "This is Jake, poppet," Bill explained in a soft voice. "He's a good friend of mine, there's no need to be frightened of him."

Bill's assurances did not persuade Amy to remove her face from his jacket, but she did sneak a peak at the man who'd frightened her so. Then she buried her nose back in her grandfather's shoulder.

Seeing that he wasn't going to convince her, Bill sent an apologetic look in Jake's direction and set Amy down. She gave Jake a skittish glance that was eerily like Rebecca's before running off to the kitchen.

"Sorry about that," Bill said. "Amy is very shy. She's leery of strangers."

Jake's face hardened as he imagined any number of grisly reasons why the little girl would be so frightened. "Why, what happened to her?"

"Not what you're thinking," Bill hastily assured him. "Amy was never abused or beaten, nothing like that. She's just had a lot of changes in her young life. Amy was still a baby, only a year and a half old, when her father died. Rebecca had to go out to work and Amy was in a child-care center during the day. Then there was the move from Chicago here to Washington. That's a lot for a child to handle. Amy's way of coping is to retreat into herself until she feels safe or secure enough to face a situation. She's just got a very cautious nature."

"She must have gotten that from her mother," Jake murmured.

"Actually Rebecca was very reckless as a child. She was constantly getting into scrapes, never looking before leaping. She's responsible for most of these white hairs I have, I can tell you."

Rebecca reckless? Jake liked the idea. "What changed her?"

"I'm not sure. Experience, I suppose." Bill took a moment to settle himself into the reading chair Amy had previously occupied before saying, "I have to tell you that when I walked in here, you looked almost as surprised to see Amy as she was to see you."

"Amy wasn't quite what I expected," Jake admitted. "She doesn't look much like Rebecca."

"Not the way Rebecca looks now, perhaps. But Amy looks very much like Rebecca did at the same age."

"Really?" Jake was clearly surprised. "But Amy's so..."

"So...what?" Rebecca demanded from the doorway, ready to jump to her daughter's defense. She knew how much careless words could hurt a child. She could still hear Ted calling Amy an ugly duckling, and she could still remember being called plain when she was a little girl herself. "Before you say another word, I'd better warn you that Amy's already told me she met the man who growls like a bear. I thought I told you to stay away from her, Jake."

"Down, girl, down," Jake teased her, holding his hands up in surrender. "I didn't attack your little girl. Our paths happened to cross here in the study."

"That's right, I can vouch for that," Bill attested. "Jake walked in while Amy was sitting in my leather chair. You know how she loves to curl up in it and tell stories to Pinkie."

"Pinkie?" Jake repeated.

"That's her stuffed toy." Bill held up the Pink Panther stuffed animal that had fallen to the side of the chair. "I got it for her on her last birthday. She usually carries it with her all the time. I'd better return Pinkie to Amy before she starts to worry."

"I'm warning you, Jake. I won't have Amy being upset," Rebecca said as soon as her father had left the study.

"Didn't you hear Bill say that Amy surprised me as much as I surprised her?"

"Amy only surprised you because she didn't fit your preconceived notions of what a little girl should look like," Rebecca retorted somewhat bitterly.

"I'm hardly an expert on what little girls should look like," he pointed out. "But if that's your fancy way of saying that her appearance surprised me, then you're absolutely right. For one thing, I wasn't expecting her to be wearing glasses. She seems so little."

"She'll be four in a few months, but she's small for her age. Not that there's anything wrong with that."

Jake wouldn't have dared say there was anything wrong, not when he was faced with a fierce tigress defending her young. The problem was, Jake wanted Rebecca to be a tigress in bed, not in a parental discussion. Fantasizing about having Rebecca in bed naturally distracted him from their current conversation. He'd preferred that to a discussion about kids any day.

Rebecca narrowed her eyes at the distinctly satisfied smile on Jake's lips. What was he up to now? "I told you that Amy is shy, that she's afraid of strangers," she reminded him.

"Yes, you did." Jake regretfully reined in his imagination and returned his attention to the present. "Your father explained why she's so shy."

His answer did not please her. Chances were that her father's explanation might well have included his theory about Amy needing a father figure. Rebecca decided she'd better dispel that fallacy immediately.

"It just takes Amy a long time to get to know someone. Of course she's lucky to already have such great father figures in her grandfather and her uncle, my older brother Kent."

"I thought Bill said Kent was in Philadelphia."

"That's right, he is. But Amy still talks to him on the phone."

Jake didn't look any more convinced of the benefits of a long-distance call than her father or brother had, Rebecca noted with irritation. What was it about men that made them all band together? "Amy has all the attention she needs."

"What about you, Rebecca?" Jake asked her in a soft voice. "What about what you need?"

"Let's just leave my needs out of this, shall we?"

He reached out and ran his fingers down her cheek. "I suppose that means you don't want to talk about the kiss we shared last night, either." He spoke with mocking wistfulness.

"That's right."

"Mmm, that's fine with me." He brushed his thumb over her parted lips. "We do seem to communicate better when we don't talk."

"Stop that." She hoped he couldn't hear how breathless she was. There was no doubting it, Jake was a pro at this form of seduction. Her legs were shaky as she stepped away from him.

"Something bothering you?" he inquired.

Some*one* was bothering her, and he knew it. "I'm fine," she informed him. To herself she added the observation that she would be much better once Jake Fletcher finished his research and moved on. Until then, things could get very dicey!

Four

After a restless night spent pondering the subject, Jake decided that the surest way to break through Rebecca's defenses was through her daughter. It made sense. Rebecca was obviously very attached to Amy. All he had to do was win the kid over to his side and he'd have it made.

Jake initiated his new battle plan the next morning. Rebecca and Amy had already eaten an early breakfast upstairs. Now that Rebecca had gone to work, Amy was in the kitchen with Dorothy while the housekeeper prepared breakfast for the two men. Jake realized he had little chance of getting to know Rebecca's daughter with her hiding in the kitchen and him eating in the dining room. That was the first thing to be changed.

"You know, Bill, there's no need for your housekeeper to go through all this trouble on my behalf." Jake indicated the elegant place settings on the mahogany dining room table. "Unless you're usually this formal for breakfast?"

"Not at all. I usually eat breakfast in the kitchen," Bill admitted.

"Then what are we doing out here?"

Bill chuckled. "You're right."

They met Dorothy on the other side of the swinging door leading into the kitchen. "Where are you two going?" the housekeeper demanded. "Breakfast's almost ready."

"We're going to eat at the table in here," Bill said.

Dorothy frowned her disapproval.

"Now, Dorothy..." Bill began in a conciliatory voice.

"Blame it on me, Dorothy," Jake inserted. "It smells so good in here that I couldn't resist."

"Hmm, I doubt if my cooking is the only thing you can't resist," Dorothy retorted, with a meaningful look in Jake's direction that said *I know what you're up to.*

Recognizing Dorothy's challenge, Jake calmly returned the housekeeper's stare.

Their face-off ended with Dorothy nodding her head with grudging acceptance. Jake had just passed the first test. "Well, if you're gonna sit in my kitchen, then you'd better set the table over there," she said gruffly. "No sense using the fine china. The regular plates are in that cabinet to the right of the sink."

Test number two, Jake thought to himself with amusement. Was this one meant to see how well he obeyed orders? But there was an even tougher test ahead—Amy. She was seated in front of a small worktable at the far end of the kitchen. She'd been drawing a picture when he and Bill had first walked into the kitchen, but she'd abandoned her crayons and was now eyeing Jake with naked distrust.

Jake tried smiling at her, but that didn't work. What should he do? Ignore her and wait until she made the first move? Talk to her? It wasn't like him to hesitate like this, but he didn't want to make a mistake. So he stood there, with the plates in his hands, staring at Amy as warily as she was staring at him.

Luckily Bill came to their rescue. "How's my poppet this morning?" he asked Amy. "Busy at work already? What are you drawing today, a picture for me?"

As Amy ran into the shelter of her grandfather's arms, Jake stole a look at the drawing she'd been working on. It was obviously a person, the odd assortment of stick arms and legs told him that much. A very tall person, taller than the house she'd drawn. He looked at Amy again and then back at the picture. Something told him that she'd been drawing him. The likeness wasn't very flattering, he noted wryly.

Amy didn't speak to him throughout breakfast. She barely spoke at all. Jake, too, remained quiet. He just observed. When Dorothy sat down and joined them for a second cup of coffee, she reached out and tickled Amy, who was sitting on Bill's lap. The little girl giggled and squirmed.

She's got Rebecca's smile, Jake thought to himself. The kind of smile that caught you by surprise and made you want to see it again. His expression softened.

A short while later, Amy slipped from her grandfather's lap and, after giving Jake a wary glance, returned to her drawing. The worktable was closest to him, and Jake was well aware that her move showed a measure of trust. It was a small step, but it gave him an incredible sense of relief. He must have just passed test number one in Amy's book.

Bill later confirmed it after they left the kitchen. "I knew you'd win Amy over."

"I wouldn't exactly call it winning her over." Jake's earlier frustration had returned. "She still looks at me as if I were the enemy."

"She just needs to get used to you. Give it time. Look at it this way, at least today she didn't run away from you. In fact, Amy felt safe enough to continue her drawing while you were still in the room."

"Patience has never been my strong point," Jake murmured.

"If you want something badly enough, I've got no doubt that you'll do whatever it takes to get it—even if that means developing patience," Bill returned.

Jake did work at improving his patience, and by the end of the week Amy no longer gave him those long distrustful looks. He and the little girl weren't close yet, but she'd begun to accept his presence.

Rebecca was another matter entirely. Where before Amy had frozen when he'd entered a room, now Rebecca was the one who acted like a scalded cat. Jake told himself not to rush Rebecca, but it was difficult when all he wanted to do was take her in his arms. Actually, he wanted to do more than just that! He wanted to make love to her, he wanted to caress every inch of her. He wanted to see those smoky-blue eyes of hers darken with passion. He wanted to see her lips all moist and parted, ready for his kiss. The bottom line was that he'd never desired a woman as much as he desired her.

At times Jake wasn't any more pleased with the discovery than she was. He certainly hadn't planned on returning to Washington and falling prey to a woman with a ready-made family. The situation was hardly ideal. These additional entanglements only complicated things. They got in the way of what he wanted—Rebecca . . . in his bed.

Jake also worried about the speculative way Bill occasionally looked at him, as if sizing him up as son-in-law material. Jake didn't know how to deal with that, so he deliberately ignored it. He tried using the rationalization that in the end he and Bill wanted the same thing for Rebecca— her happiness. At the moment they just had different views on how to accomplish that goal.

But last night Jake lay in bed, staring a hole into the ceiling. His desire for Rebecca wasn't the only thing keeping him awake; now he was beginning to wrestle with a guilty conscience. Bill had invited him into his house and here he was, lusting after his daughter. On the other hand, Bill had gone out of his way to show his approval of Jake's courting Rebecca.

But maybe that was because Bill thought the thing would end in marriage, Jake reminded himself. Personally, he didn't know where it would end. How could he think about an ending when things hadn't even begun?

He was struck by the irony of the situation. He'd gotten himself involved with the very thing he'd avoided most of his life—a family. Dealing with fathers, kids and housekeepers was all new to him. But he was determined to succeed. And the smoldering passion he occasionally caught in Rebecca's eyes was enough to give him hope.

She'd been looking at him that way a moment ago when she'd first walked into the study and found him there, but the mask was back in place now.

Rebecca took a calming breath. Even after a week she still hadn't gotten used to walking into a room and finding Jake sitting there. He looked great in a pair of crisp blue jeans and a blue shirt. The problem was that Jake looked better to her each time she saw him.

Say something, she ordered herself. *Don't just stand here like an idiot. Act natural. Don't let him see he's getting to you.*

"How is the research going? Are you just about done?" she asked, hoping to find some light at the end of this particular tunnel.

Jake smiled before replying. "I'm just getting started."

Great, Rebecca morosely thought to herself. *He's just getting started, and I'm about ready to cave in!* It was time she called in some reinforcements. It was time she accepted that dinner invitation from Steve Fisher, the accountant who'd asked her out on several occasions. The thought restored some of her confidence. Surely she could handle Jake. But for how much longer? "This research of yours seems to be taking you a long time to complete."

"That's because I don't always know what I'm looking for until I find it."

"Sounds to me like a strange way of doing it."

"How are you used to doing it?" His provocative question was laced with sexual overtones.

You walked right into that one, she derided herself. Deciding that her best course of action would be to ignore his double entendre, she took his question at face value. "I do my research by the bibliographic method."

He raised an eyebrow at her reply. "Sounds interesting."

"You should try it some time. It might speed up your research."

"I'll keep that in mind," he promised. The wicked gleam in his eyes gave her the definite impression that he wouldn't be applying her suggestion to his work, however. "I'd like to speed things up. Of course there's something to be said for going slowly, too. Gives you time to enjoy every step. Wouldn't want to miss anything in the rush for ... completion."

Rebecca nervously licked her dry lips and wiped her damp hands on her cotton slacks. There was no doubt about it, Jake was a master of verbal foreplay. She was actually shaking. Definitely time to make that call to Steve. Hopefully, a night out in the company of another man would mitigate Jake's effect on her.

As Rebecca got ready for her date later that evening, she couldn't help worrying about Jake's reaction when he found out she was going out with someone else.

"Not that I care what he thinks," she loftily informed her reflection in the bathroom mirror. "I just didn't want him causing a scene, that's all."

"Who you talking to, Mommy?" Amy asked with wide-eyed curiosity as she pushed open the unlatched bathroom door.

Rebecca blushed. "No one, pumpkin."

"Can I talk to no one, too?" Amy ingeniously inquired.

Rebecca hugged her. Oh, to be a child again. Everything had been so simple then. Unlike now, when things got more complicated by the hour.

Up until the moment Steve picked her up, Rebecca was worried that Jake would make a scene. In fact, he reacted quite calmly—too calmly. He was even polite to Steve, asking him questions, smiling. Jake was definitely up to something, and Rebecca spent most of her evening with Steve wondering exactly what it was Jake had up his sleeve this time.

Meanwhile, Jake spent most of his evening brooding in the study. Bill had gone out to an alumni dinner at the university and Dorothy was upstairs putting Amy to bed. Left alone with his own thoughts, Jake reviewed what he'd learned about Rebecca's date. The guy was divorced with two kids of his own. A family man. Three-piece suit, respectable background, house in the suburbs. Jake gritted his teeth and reminded himself that Rebecca's last-minute date with Fisher was only an act of rebellion. Even so, he waited up for her.

She was home by ten forty-five. There was no sign of Fisher when she entered the house.

"Have a nice evening?" Jake inquired. He was standing guard in the front foyer.

"Very nice."

His hands were jammed into the back pockets of his jeans, as if they had to be restrained from reaching out and shaking her. "Known the guy long?"

Rebecca's chin lifted, and mutinous anger glinted in her blue eyes. "What are you? My keeper?"

"No. I plan on being your lover. You might as well get used to the idea."

"That's not an idea, it's a delusion!" she retorted, infuriated by his outrageous assertion.

Bill walked in the front door at that point. Having heard Rebecca's angry voice, if not her exact words, he murmured indulgently, "You two at it again?"

Rebecca gave both men a blistering look before pivoting and marching upstairs.

"Your daughter certainly does have a temper," Jake noted.

"I did warn you."

"So you did." Jake grinned. "Are the plans still on for tomorrow morning?"

Bill nodded. "Amy and I will be making breakfast for Rebecca as a Mother's Day surprise. Are you sure you still want to join in?"

Since Dorothy had Mother's Day off, Bill and Amy planned on bringing Rebecca breakfast in bed. Of course as soon as he'd heard about the plans, Jake had counted himself in on the deal.

"Yes, I still want to join in," Jake stated. He just hoped Rebecca didn't toss the breakfast tray at him!

By seven the next morning Jake, Bill and Amy were in the kitchen whipping up a batch of waffles.

"I didn't know you could actually make these from scratch," Jake said. "I thought they only came frozen out of a box."

"Once you've tasted the real thing, you'll never go back to that frozen stuff again," Bill maintained.

Eager to get started, Amy impatiently wrinkled her nose.

Jake watched her maneuver with some amusement. She looked like a little rabbit when she screwed her face up like that.

Amy tugged on Bill's pant leg. "Can I squish the eggs, Grandpa?" she asked shyly.

"Sure, poppet." Bill cracked the eggs on the side of a mixing bowl. "Here you go." He set the bowl on the table and handed her a mixing spoon. "Climb on up here." He held out a chair for her.

In her enthusiasm Amy stirred so fast that one of the eggs slid over the edge of the shallow metal bowl and landed with a plop on Jake's sneakers. Amy's eyes widened. Dropping the spoon she put both hands over her mouth.

Even through the thick lenses of her glasses, Jake could see tears gathering. "It's okay," he reassured her. "I saw that egg jump right out of the bowl. We're lucky my shoe caught it before it got away, huh?"

There was a moment of silence during which time Jake wondered what had made him concoct such a ridiculous story. The kid would think he was nuts!

Sure enough, Amy was looking at him doubtfully. "Are you mad at me?"

Jake shook his head.

"The shoe caughted-ed the egg?"

Jake nodded.

Amy smiled. It was a shy smile, and it didn't last long, but it was definitely a smile. "I wish I had shoes like that."

Jake finally felt he was making progress. This kid stuff wasn't so hard after all. Now all he had to do was show Rebecca how well he got along with her daughter. Jake's confidence remained high, despite the fact that he burned two helpings of waffles and Bill had to take over as waffle monitor.

The three of them were on their way upstairs—Jake carrying the white wicker bed tray, Amy carrying her stuffed toy, Pinkie—when the phone rang.

"You two go on up or the waffles will get cold," Bill instructed Jake and Amy. "I'll answer the phone."

When they got upstairs Jake let Amy do all the talking. "Sshhh, we're not supposta wake my mommy, it's supposta be a surprise." Amy carefully opened the door leading into the apartment and Jake got his first view of Rebecca's private domain.

Homey, comfortable, warm—those were the impressions that first hit him. Unlike the downstairs, which was always kept in immaculate order by Dorothy, up here there was a more lived-in look. A few toys were strewn around the floor in one corner, some open magazines were spread out on the coffee table, and a pair of high-heeled shoes lay on their side near the front door. The floor plan was open and practical with the living room, dining area and kitchen merging into one another without benefit of separating walls.

"Come on," Amy whispered.

Jake followed her down a short hall that branched off to the right.

Amy opened the bedroom door and ran inside. "Surprise!"

Rebecca snuggled into the covers, savoring those last few seconds of the wonderful dream she'd been having.

"Mommy, wake up!" Amy tugged on the covers.

Rebecca responded by tugging on Amy and bringing the little girl tumbling down onto the bed. It was a morning ritual. Rebecca wrestled with her daughter and kissed her until she squealed.

Jake stood appreciating the scene. He liked the idea of grabbing Rebecca and tumbling her onto the covers, kissing her until she squealed, or better yet surrendered. He also liked the way Rebecca's nightgown was almost falling off one shoulder. It was pink and of some sort of silky material that clung in all the right places. He stood there enjoying the view, as he had the first time he'd ever seen her.

He wasn't the only one experiencing déjà vu. Even though she wasn't wearing her contacts, Rebecca could see that the man standing at the foot of her bed was taller than her father. Which meant—

"Breakfast is served," Jake announced.

Rebecca felt like sinking under the bed, or at the very least pulling the covers over her head. She was hardly in a state to be receiving visitors. Her long hair was coming free of its loose braid, her face was flushed with embarrassment, and her nightgown, which had been fine for an early-morning visit from her daughter and father, was too revealing for a visit from Jake. Actually the sleepwear was perfectly respectable, Jake was the one who made her feel...what? Sexy? On Mother's Day?

Disconcerted, Rebecca groped for the pair of glasses on the bedside table. They didn't provide much protection, but she did feel a little less vulnerable. Until Jake said, "You still look sexy, even with the glasses."

What was he? A mind reader? "Where's my father?" Rebecca demanded. How could her parent have let Jake waltz into her bedroom like this?

"Bill had a phone call. He'll be up in a few minutes."

Impatient with the adult conversation, Amy tugged on Rebecca's arm. "Look, Mommy. Waffles! I got to squish the eggs, and one fell on the man's magic shoes, and the shoe caughted-ed it. Can I get magic shoes like that?"

Rebecca had to laugh at Amy's excited rapid-fire delivery. "Slow down, honey. What magic shoes?"

"Those ones." Amy pointed to Jake's sneakers. "He said they was magic," she added in a whisper.

Rebecca looked at Jake with curious eyes. She wouldn't have expected him to have come up with such an ingenious story. But then Jake was a storyteller by nature. Making things up was part of his trade. Believing him also came naturally, especially to females—even little ones.

For herself, Rebecca could easily believe that Jake meant it when he looked at her as if she were the only woman in the world for him. But believing it wouldn't make it true.

Feeling the need for additional protection Rebecca said, "Amy, honey, hand Mommy that sweater over there, would you?"

"Don't cover yourself up on my account," Jake said in a sexy drawl.

"I'm not," Rebecca denied. "It's chilly in here."

"Is that right? Funny, I'm real warm."

The heat from Jake's gaze was enough to start a bonfire. He caressed her with his eyes, running them over every inch of exposed skin. His approval was obvious.

"Here, Mommy." Amy handed her the sweater.

Rebecca hurriedly tugged it on and buttoned the oversize buttons.

"You ready for breakfast now?" Jake inquired dryly.

Rebecca nodded and leaned forward to take the tray from him.

"No, you don't," he admonished her. "No fighting over the tray. You wouldn't want your breakfast to spill all over the bed, now would you? Put some pillows behind your back, and make yourself comfortable."

Rebecca reluctantly did as he ordered.

Jake set the tray on her lap and then sat next to her, just a few inches from her thigh. His weight caused the mattress to dip, which in turn rolled Rebecca even closer to him.

Meanwhile Amy crawled over Rebecca's feet and curled up on the other side of the double bed. "Eat it, Mommy. It's good for you."

"That's right, Rebecca, it's good for you." What Jake really meant was *I'm* good for you—and he made sure she knew it.

Rebecca busied herself pouring maple syrup over her waffles. She used her fingertip to catch the last drop as it hung from the rim of the serving pitcher. But before she could lick the sweet stickiness from her finger, Jake captured her hand and did the job himself.

"Mmm, good," he murmured.

Too good, Rebecca thought to herself. The feel of his tongue on her fingertip reminded her how much she'd missed his touch. Pleasure raced through her, leaving her shaken and uncertain.

"Mommy," Amy piped up. "Pinkie wants some syrup, too."

Grateful for the interruption, Rebecca snatched her hand away. "Has Pinkie been good today?"

Amy nodded.

"Okay, Pinkie, here you go." Rebecca held her finger out to the stuffed animal, even though there was no longer any syrup left on it—Jake had done an excellent job of cleaning up. He'd also done an excellent job of arousing feelings she wished had been left alone. She was finding it increasingly difficult to remember that Jake was merely amusing himself with her.

Rebecca's thoughts were troubled as she finally took her first forkful of waffles.

"Mommy, you look sad. How come? Does it taste bad?"

"No, honey. The waffles are real good," Rebecca reassured her. "Didn't you have any?"

Amy nodded. "Me and Grandpa sneaked some before."

"What about Jake?" Rebecca found herself asking.

"I'm still hungry," he answered. "Want to share?"

"There's only one fork."

"You said people are supposta share, Mommy," Amy reminded her.

"You heard her," Jake seconded. "People are supposta share."

Amy waited expectantly until Rebecca gave in and handed Jake a forkful of waffles.

"Aren't you going to feed it to me?" he inquired.

"I'm going to throw it at you in a second," she warned him under her breath.

Jake wisely took the fork and fed himself.

"I'm gonna go look for Grandpa now," Amy suddenly announced.

"Wait, Amy!" Rebecca said, but her daughter had already scampered off the bed and out of the room.

"There goes your chaperon," Jake murmured mockingly.

Rebecca gave him a look filled with exasperation. "I wish you'd stop playing these games of seduction."

"Who's playing games?"

"You are."

"I don't play games, Rebecca. I don't have the patience." The flare of passion in his dark eyes reflected the fact that it took all of his patience and self-control to refrain from joining her under the covers.

Distracted, she wailed, "Why are you doing this? There are plenty of willing women in Washington. Why don't you go after one of them and leave me alone?"

"I already told you, Rebecca. Other women don't interest me. You do."

"Only because I'm a challenge for you," she retorted. "I know how you operate. You're a loner looking for some fun for the brief time you'll be in town. I've done my research on you. You never stay in one place for long, and you're never seen with the same woman twice."

"I've been seen with you more than twice," he pointed out.

"I'm talking about women you've gone out with. *I've* never gone out with you."

"Not yet, but you will."

"Haven't you heard a word I've said?" she demanded.

"I've heard every word you've said. And I know why you've said them. I understand your protectiveness; you don't want Amy hurt, you don't want your father hurt, you don't want yourself hurt. Now it's up to me to show you that I don't intend to hurt any of you."

"I don't want you to show me anything."

"No?" With slow deliberation he first removed the bed tray, then leaned closer to remove her glasses. "You don't want me to show you what kissing you like this—" his lips caressed her cheek "—does to me?"

She shook her head.

"You don't want me to show you how much I want to hold you like this?" He slid his arms around her.

She shook her head again, less forcefully this time. He moved forward slightly. His mouth was so close. Was he going to kiss her?

It was more a teasing seduction than a kiss. His lips lightly brushed hers, back and forth—skimming but never settling. He formed the words against her mouth. "You don't . . . want me . . . to show you . . . how special . . . this attraction is?"

"No." She wasn't sure if she was answering his question or protesting the increasing intimacy of his hold because it felt so good. Too good. She had to stop this while she still could. "Jake, no!"

He allowed her to pull away from him. "What *do* you want, Rebecca?"

"I want you to leave so that I can get dressed."

Jake had his own reasons for obeying her request. Rebecca wasn't the only one afraid of starting something. Having her so close to him, holding her in his arms, kissing her—all while she was lying there in bed—was more temptation than he could take. Any more of this fooling around, and he wouldn't be able to stop. Although they were in the right place, it wasn't the right time for making love, not when her father or her daughter could walk in any minute. When he made her his, Jake wanted all the time in the world to savor the pleasure. And he would make her his, of that he was sure.

Five

Left alone with her own unsettling thoughts, Rebecca jumped out of bed and marched into the bathroom. At least there she could mutter to herself without fear of being overheard.

Turning on the water, she irritably wondered how many other women had been forced to take a cold shower thanks to Jake's teasing seduction. Very few, she decided an instant later as she remembered the powerful magic of his touch. Most would no doubt give in to his caresses and welcome him into their bed without a second thought.

Rebecca sighed. As she sliced her hand through the pulsing stream of water, testing the temperature, it occurred to her that she hadn't always been this cautious. She never used to test the waters before jumping in, be it into the shower or into a relationship. But that recklessness had gotten her burned, and she'd learned from her mistakes.

Why did a rambler like Jake Fletcher have to be the one to make her feel like this—all hot and bothered, all warm and susceptible? Why couldn't it have been someone with a strong sense of family? Someone who shared her goals in life? Rebecca adjusted the water temperature one more time before stepping into the shower. She had more questions than answers.

Downstairs, Jake was already standing beneath the chilling waters of a cold shower. Winning Rebecca was going to be tougher than he'd first anticipated, but he refused to be discouraged by the discovery. He'd learned the hard way that anything worth having was worth fighting for. And Rebecca was definitely worth having!

Just thinking about the way he'd held her in his arms, as he had a few minutes ago, made him burn with desire for her. As he lowered the water temperature yet again, Jake vowed that Rebecca was going to compensate him for every single cold shower he'd had to take since finding her in that elevator a week ago. That thought brought a smile to his face.

Rebecca still hadn't come down when Jake reappeared in the kitchen. Bill was seated at the table, sipping a cup of coffee, while Amy was drawing at her worktable.

Bill, cordial host that he was, didn't say a word about Jake's second shower of the morning. Instead he said, "Sorry that phone call took me so long. It was Dorothy. She wanted to know how things were going, make sure we were getting on all right without her. So tell me, was my daughter surprised to see you bringing her breakfast?"

"Surprised is an understatement." Jake poured himself a cup of coffee and joined Bill at the table. "Shocked is more like it."

"Mommy had to share her waffles," Amy inserted.

The little girl's comment reminded Jake that little pitchers have big ears. Or was it little *pictures* have big ears?

Whatever the phrase was, he'd have to watch what he said around her.

Looking at Amy, Jake remembered his surprise the first time he'd seen her. Big glasses, plain face, thin little arms and legs. She might not be pretty, but the kid wasn't bad. She kind of grew on you.

Jake's attention shifted from Amy to Bill. The older man had gone out of his way to make Jake feel like one of the family. Jake was only now coming to realize how much he liked the feeling. And that surprised him. He'd expected this family thing to be smothering, but instead he was actually beginning to enjoy it.

But Jake couldn't help wondering if Bill would be as supportive if he knew more about him. Jake had never told Bill about his childhood, never told him anything more than the basic facts about his burnout. Jake knew the time was rapidly coming when he'd have to talk about those things.

Jake looked back at Amy. She was such a quiet little thing, not much of a talker at all. He and Amy had that much in common at least. When he was a kid, he'd liked the sound of silence.

Noticing his houseguest's preoccupation with Amy, Bill decided that this might be the perfect time to slip upstairs for a quick father-daughter chat with Rebecca. "I'll just go see what's keeping Rebecca," he murmured.

Bill's departure left Jake with the sudden realization that this was the first time he'd ever really been alone with Amy. Dorothy, Bill or Rebecca had always been around before. Jake told himself it was stupid to think there was any difference, but he suddenly felt awkward. The silence was no longer reassuring, it was deafening. The only noise came from the hum of the refrigerator, and that sounded like the roar of a jet engine.

Across the kitchen, Amy had stopped coloring and was sitting perfectly still, staring at *his* shoes.

Her interest gave him a much needed topic of conversation. "These shoes were pretty smart to catch that egg, huh?"

"Do you..." Amy paused shyly. "Do you know any more stories 'bout magic shoes?"

Jake didn't, but he could certainly make up some in a hurry. "Do you want to hear a story now?"

Amy nodded, her glasses slipping down her tiny nose.

"Okay. Once upon a time..." Once he got started Jake found that he was really getting into his role of storyteller. With each sentence he began adding more embellishment until he was really on a roll. "And then this big monster came out of—Hey, Amy! Wait! Where are you going?"

As soon as he'd mentioned monsters, the little girl had jumped out of her seat and gone racing out of the kitchen, crying.

It didn't take long after that for the kitchen door to swing open again. "What did you say to her?" Rebecca demanded angrily. Dressed in a pair of khaki slacks and a purple blouse, she was glaring at him with all the outrage of a protective mother.

Jake glared right back at her. He didn't like being on the defensive. "I was just telling her a story."

"About what?"

"You can take that look off your face, I wasn't telling her anything X-rated. Nothing with sex or violence in it, nothing that wasn't suitable for general audiences."

"Let me be the judge of that. What was the story about?"

"The shoes that catch eggs."

Rebecca was clearly surprised. "That's it?"

He nodded. "She asked me to tell her a story about the shoes, so I did. But when I got to the part about the monsters, she ran—"

"Wait a minute. What are monsters doing in a story about shoes?"

Jake said, "I thought monsters were supposed to be in all kids' stories."

"Well, you thought wrong! Amy is terrified of monsters. She's even been having nightmares about them."

"How was I supposed to know that? You should have told me."

How like him to put the blame on her. Unintentionally her voice rose to a yell. "I told you to stay away from Amy!"

Jake responded by getting angry, too. "You've told me a lot of things you don't mean!"

Now they were both yelling.

"What are you talking about?" she demanded in a quieter voice.

"I'm talking about the way you melted in my arms upstairs a little while ago."

"I did not *melt*!" At least not visibly, she added to herself. She'd made sure of that.

Jake dismissed her protest. "When are you going to get your stubborn head out of the sand and face facts?"

Bill's arrival in the kitchen prevented Rebecca from answering.

Seeing the worried question in his daughter's eyes, Bill quickly reassured her. "Amy's fine, but it sounds like you two need a referee in here."

"We don't need a referee," Rebecca denied. "Our little discussion is over."

"No, it's not." Jake looked grimly determined. "We need to talk."

"Perhaps you two should talk outside," Bill suggested. "That way Amy won't hear all the shouting and commotion. Besides, the back patio is lovely this time of year."

"I don't have anything else to say to Jake."

"Then you can just listen. Come on." Jake put his hands on her shoulders and marched her through the open French doors leading onto the brick patio.

Bill closed the doors after them and crossed his fingers for good luck before rejoining Amy.

Outside Jake began, "I think there are a few things we need to clear up here." He'd come to a halt next to some potted tree roses. The heady floral scent filled the air, but both Jake and Rebecca were too immersed in their showdown to be aware of it.

"Earlier you said that you'd been doing research on me. What exactly did you mean by that?" Jake demanded.

"I meant what I said. Someone at the library gave me a few articles that had been written about you. Don't worry, nothing I read was unexpected."

"No?" A minute later Rebecca found herself in his arms. "Are you accusing me of being predictable?" he questioned softly.

"I'm not accusing you of anything." Her voice was unsteady.

"Yes, you are. You've already accused me of being a loner who never stays in one place for long and who's never seen with the same woman twice. Isn't that the way you put it?"

"Are you denying it?" Half of her wished he would, while the other half was afraid of what his denial could mean.

"What if I were?"

Impatient with his evasiveness, she freed herself from his hold. "Why can't you ever give me a straight answer?"

Jake was equally impatient. "You want a straight answer, fine, I'll give you one! Let's start with me not staying in one place very long. I lived and worked here in Washington for six years before I became a writer, or have you conveniently forgotten that fact?"

"And as soon as you became a writer you couldn't wait to get away from here," she retorted. "Since then you've never stayed in one place very long, or put down anything even resembling roots. You've become the proverbial rolling stone.''

''I had my reasons.''

She waited a moment, stupidly hoping that he'd tell her what his reasons were. She should have known better. Loners not only kept to themselves, they kept their secrets to themselves as well. Feeling unreasonably disappointed, she lashed out. ''Since I don't know anything about those reasons, I can't even begin to figure you out! All I know is what I see, and I see a man who's made a point of avoiding commitments, either to a place or to a person.''

''You see what you want to see,'' he stated impatiently. ''Did you ever consider that maybe I move around so much because I'm looking for something?'' He paused for a moment, and when he spoke again, his voice was softer. ''I once told you that I don't always know what I'm looking for until I find it. That's how I feel about you.'' He reached out to cup her cheek with his hand. ''I didn't know what I was looking for until I met you. Now I know.'' He tipped her chin up, compelling her to look at him. ''I want you. And I think you want me, too.''

Rebecca was almost afraid to breathe. She'd grown tired of denying her feelings. She did want Jake. And she knew her eyes revealed that fact. It would be so easy to lose herself in the passion she saw mirrored in his eyes. But it would be so hard being left behind when he moved on to someone else. She needed more than passion; she needed something that would last. Hard as it was, she stepped away from him.

''Jake, this isn't going to work. There's more at stake here than just physical attraction. I've got a daughter to consider. I'm not in the market for a fling. And unlike you, I *do* know what I want before I find it. I want someone capable of making a commitment and sticking to it, someone who has his priorities straight. I want a man who won't sacrifice relationships at the altar of his career, a man who values family."

"What makes you think I'm not that man?" he countered.

"Come on. You? A family man?"

He was irked by her disbelief. "Stranger things have happened."

Rebecca suddenly realized that the more she denied it, the more he would take her words as a challenge. And Jake never walked away from a challenge—she'd learned that much about him. A change of tactics was obviously called for here. Maybe if she stopped running, Jake would stop pursuing. Maybe once Jake had a taste of family life, he'd find out for himself that it wasn't to his liking.

Her silence made Jake's irritation grow. "All right, so I don't have a strong family background like your friend Fisher, but that isn't necessarily a drawback. In fact, it could be an advantage. Never having had a real family might make me appreciate what other people take for granted."

Here was her chance to find out something about his background. "If you didn't have a *real* family, what did you have?"

"Trouble. The truth is that I didn't come from your average all-American home; I wasn't one of 2.5 children who lived with my happy parents in the suburbs with a dog in the yard and a station wagon in the garage. I grew up in the city where they made the station wagons. Detroit."

When he stopped there, Rebecca was sure he wasn't going to tell her anything. Still some nugget of hope made her say, "Go on."

To her surprise, he did. "I was an only child. My mother died when I was seven or eight. My father was bitter about her 'deserting us', as he put it. As if she had a choice," Jake muttered grimly. His face was dark, brooding.

Rebecca trembled. Her own mother had died when she was fourteen; she knew how much it hurt. Suddenly she wasn't sure she'd done the right thing in asking Jake about his childhood. It was obviously a painful subject for him.

"My father was no good at handling a kid, so he let me run wild. When you grow up on the streets, you learn to fend for yourself at an early age." Jake shrugged. "I guess that made me something of a loner."

Rebecca could see how it would. It was disheartening to discover that Jake's loner days went that far back. Somehow it made the likelihood of his ever settling down that much slimmer.

"Can't you see how little we have in common?" she said.

"Because you're a respectable Georgetown lady and I'm just a guy from the streets?" He sounded angry.

"No. I'm not talking about our pasts, I'm talking about our future. We want different things."

"You say you want a family man. All right, I say show me the merits of family life. Who knows? Maybe you'll convince me."

She doubted that, but she knew that putting it to the test was the only way she could convince herself that Jake wasn't the man for her.

Rebecca spent the rest of the day reviewing her options. By the time she went to bed, she'd reached a decision. She would stop running from Jake. Without the challenge of the chase, she believed that he'd soon grow bored and lose interest.

Who knows? she thought to herself as she switched off the lights. *Maybe when Jake encounters the new you, he'll be the one who goes running in the opposite direction.* The thought should have cheered her more than it did.

Rebecca awoke the next morning with a firm resolve to stick to her new plan. Feeling the need for a morale booster, she decided against the tailored blouse and skirt she usually wore in favor of a softer dress. The summery cotton print made her feel fresh and feminine.

Unfortunately it didn't take long for her to feel wrinkled and wilted after using public transportation to get to work. The bus and the Metro were about as relaxing as being propped up in a sardine can. Add a morning of cataloging policy meetings, and you had the beginnings of a headache.

By twelve o'clock Rebecca was ready for a break. She was also ready to eat the bagged lunch she'd just retrieved from the staff refrigerator. She was not ready to see Jake lounging against the doorway leading to the cataloging office.

He looked wonderful, as always. He was wearing dark slacks and a dark red, short-sleeved shirt. Objectively she knew that Jake was not getting handsomer every hour. It just felt that way, and it wasn't even due to any effort on his part.

Jake wasn't the type of man who put much store in the new masculine pastime of "looking good." No blow-dried haircuts, no trendy clothes or successful designer labels for him. He didn't need any of those surface trappings. He had something much more attractive—confidence in himself.

When Rebecca finally pulled her eyes away from Jake, she noticed that everyone else's eyes were bouncing between her and her unexpected visitor. No doubt they were all waiting for the fireworks to start, Rebecca thought in sudden irritation. Well, she wasn't going to provide the entertainment today. Besides, the time had come for her to stop running.

"I'm going to lunch, Nancy," she quickly informed her co-worker.

"Have fun," Nancy murmured with a grin.

Jake waited for Rebecca to come to him. He'd noticed the dress right off and nodded his approval. "Nice," he murmured with a naughty look at her legs. "Very nice."

Rebecca tried to squeeze past him, but he was blocking the doorway very effectively. Determined to get Jake away before he could say or do anything else to set tongues wagging, Rebecca put her hand on his chest and backed him out into the hallway.

It was the first time she'd ever touched him voluntarily, and she found the experience disturbingly enjoyable. Her fingers lingered, savoring the warmth of his skin through the thin cotton of his shirt, and her curiosity took flight as she imagined Jake without the shirt.

Jake smiled as if he knew her thoughts. "You know, I just love aggressive women."

She flushed but didn't remove her hand. At least not immediately. "What are you doing here?"

"I've come to take you away from all this." He held up the paper bag he was carrying. "Lunch. Outside. In the fresh air. It's a beautiful day, much too nice to stay inside hunched over books."

"I agree."

"What? Do my ears deceive me?" he questioned in disbelief as she grabbed him by the arm and hustled him down the hallway. "I can't be hearing you right. I actually thought you said you agreed with me about something."

"I did agree, but I'll stop if you're going to gloat about it."

"As if I'd dare."

"You'd dare anything."

"Ah, the lady's beginning to know me."

And beginning to like him, Rebecca was startled to realize. Or maybe she was finally *allowing* herself to like him. Either way she'd have to be careful her feelings didn't get out of hand. But her good intentions vanished as soon as they got outside. Spring was in the air, and with it came a certain recklessness, a certain impulsiveness.

They ended up sitting on a park bench across the street from the library's main building and within sight of the Capitol's famous dome. The sidewalk and lawn were filled with government workers enjoying the midday break. It was one of those perfect May days, sunny with just a hint of a breeze—the kind that made you feel glad to be alive. Even the foraging squirrels were having a field day, happily munching the goodies being tossed their way by the alfresco lunch crowd.

After opening the paper bag he was carrying, Jake announced, "You've got a choice of pastrami on rye or roast beef on white."

"Thanks but I prefer my sandwich." She opened her own paper bag. "Avocado and cashew on French."

He looked at her in disbelief. "You're kidding, right?"

"Not at all." She took out the sandwich and showed it to him.

"You're not really going to eat that, are you?"

Rebecca nodded and took a bite, ignoring Jake's grimace. After washing it down with a sip of Perrier water, she gave him a piece of advice. "People living in glass houses, eating pastrami on rye and drinking beer, shouldn't throw stones."

"I don't live in a glass house. I live in your house."

Technically speaking, it was her father's house, but she saw no point in reminding him of that fact. It was much too nice a day to argue.

Instead she sat there, quietly enjoying the view. To the casual observer she might have appeared to be dreamily studying the Italian Renaissance style of the library's main building. After all, the architecture was much more pleasing than the modern functional lines of the library annex building where she worked. And it was true that she loved all the elaborate pillars and arches fronting the famous building. But the real truth of the matter was that she was thinking about Jake.

It was a habit she'd gotten into more and more lately. She caught herself wondering what he looked like with a face full of shaving cream, wondering if he slept on his side or on his back, wondering if he wore pajamas or slept in the nude.

"Earth to Rebecca." He waved a hand in front of her dazed eyes. "What do you see in that building that's so fascinating?"

She automatically came up with some statistics left over from the morning's cataloging meetings. "I see a collection of eighty million items that take up over five hundred miles of shelving."

Jake looked at her and then at the building. "What have you got, X-ray eyes?"

"My eyes are blue," she replied demurely.

"I noticed. I also noticed that you're not wearing your librarian glasses today."

"I've told you, I only wear them to catalog dusty old books."

"And to discourage unexpected guests who bring you breakfast in bed," he added. "But as I told you yesterday, you still looked sexy, even with the glasses."

Rebecca decided it was time to stop hemming and hawing. The gleam in his eyes told her that he expected her to be flustered by his compliment. This was the moment for the hunted to become the hunter. "You're looking pretty sexy yourself today," she declared.

His double-take made her smile. And the warmth in her eyes surprised him so much that he choked on his sandwich.

"What's the matter?" She solicitously patted him on the back. "Did it go down the wrong way?"

"I'm in shock," he croaked.

"Good thing I have first-aid training then."

Her pert reassurance threw him. He became wary. "What's going on here?"

"What do you mean, Jake?"

"You're up to something. What is it?"

"Why the third degree?" Rebecca studied him with artful candor. "Surely you've been told you're sexy before?"

"Not by a librarian."

She grinned. "How nice to be a first."

"What did you put in that Perrier water?" He eyed the bottle suspiciously.

"Nothing. Why do you ask?"

"Because you're acting very strangely all of a sudden."

"Are you complaining?"

"No, I'm just curious about this sudden turnaround."

"There's no mystery," she replied. "I gave a great deal of thought to what you said yesterday, and I decided that you're right."

Jake looked ready to choke again. "What?"

This was going better than Rebecca had expected. "You said that I should convince you of the merits of family life."

"And you're agreeing to do that?" His amazement was obvious.

"Isn't that what you wanted?" she asked with wide-eyed innocence.

"Yes."

"Good. Then the first thing you should do is check out these books at the library." She handed him a folded sheet of paper she'd pulled from her purse.

"What's this?"

"A bibliography. I told you I believe in the bibliographic method of research, remember?"

"What kind of research?" Jake asked.

"Research about family life. You'll find these books very helpful, I'm sure."

The only thing Jake was sure of was that Rebecca was up to something. But for the time being he decided to let her play out her hand. She'd stopped running—that was the most important thing. He'd figure out her game plan later.

Two hours later Jake sat in the Library of Congress Main Reading Room, surrounded by piles of books. Hardcovers, paperbacks. How to, how not to. He thumbed through them all, looking for one that would tell him what he wanted to know. But none of them made sense to him. Whatever one book said, another contradicted, giving him the impression that none of them knew what they were talking about.

He felt like a fish out of water. These parenting handbooks were mumbo jumbo to him. Checking crime statistics and ballistic reports were more up his alley than this child behavior stuff.

In the end he decided to forget the books and go back to trusting his gut instincts with Amy. The one mistake he'd made so far—talking about monsters—wasn't something that reading some book could've prevented. Experience was the best teacher. The more practice he got, the better he'd become at handling Amy. Or so he hoped.

Dorothy was vehemently punching bread dough when Jake entered the kitchen a little after three. Amy was sitting at her drawing table, finger-painting. The little girl was quieter than she'd been lately, and Jake knew he'd have to make up for lost ground. He didn't push her, just sat at the kitchen table and watched her paint.

"That looks like fun," he said with just the right amount of wistfulness.

"Did you used to play before you got old?" Amy asked him.

Dorothy quickly put a flour-covered hand up to muffle her laughter.

Jake felt all of 133.

"I never got to finger-paint," he admitted.

Amy looked shocked. "Never?"

Jake shook his head.

Amy held out a pot of bright blue paint. "You can play with mine," she offered solemnly.

Jake felt a funny twist in his heart. Must have been that pastrami and rye, he cynically told himself. Or was this kid actually getting to him?

"My friend, Trixie, is painting, too," Amy announced.

"She is?" Jake looked around the kitchen. "Where?"

"There." Amy pointed to an empty chair at the table. "I can see her, but nobody else can," she informed him proudly.

"I see," he replied.

"You see her, too?" Amy appeared surprised by this news.

"I'm not sure," he admitted. Maybe he should have gotten one of those books after all. Did they have a chapter on invisible friends?

"Trixie sees you. Are you going to play with us?"

"Sure." Jake took the pot of finger paint from Amy's little fingers. "Uh, but you're going to have to show me how this works. I've never done it before."

"You has to have an apron like Trixie and me."

Dorothy took great joy in handing Jake a frilly pinafore—pink, no less!

Seeing Jake's disgruntled expression, Amy quickly reassured him. "That's okay if you look silly. Trixie and me don't mind."

"Thanks," he murmured dryly. "That makes me feel a lot better."

"It's the only extra apron I've got," Dorothy insisted as she tied the ties around his waist. "Don't worry about getting paint on it. Pink was never my color."

"It's not exactly mine either," Jake grumbled.

"Here's your paper." Amy joined him at the big table. "Now put your fingers in the paint . . ." Amy demonstrated for him.

Seeing Jake's reluctance, Dorothy reassured him. "It washes off your hands."

"It had better," he muttered before gingerly inserting one finger into the jar of red.

"Now squish it all around," Amy instructed.

Jake gingerly wiped the red goo on the paper.

"No, bigger than that."

He painted a circle, turned it into a face with two eyes and a smile, then added a blue house, some green trees, a yellow sun. . . .

The sound of feminine laughter interrupted his artistic endeavors. Jake looked up from his masterpiece to see Rebecca standing in the kitchen doorway.

"We're playing," Amy proudly announced. "Do you want to play, too, Mommy?"

Still laughing, Rebecca shook her head.

"What's so funny?" Jake demanded as if he didn't already know.

"You are. Picasso at work." Rebecca's voice was husky with amusement. "Picasso in a pink pinafore, no less!"

He stood, eager to get rid of the ridiculous apron thing he was wearing, but his hands were still filled with paint. "Untie this," he ordered Rebecca.

"Untie this, please," she corrected him.

"Mommy always makes me say please," Amy declared.

"Someday I'm going to make Mommy say please," Jake muttered. "Okay, untie it, *please*. Are you happy now?"

Rebecca helped him out of the frilly apron.

"Are you gonna play, too, Mommy?" Amy asked again.

"Yeah, Mommy, why don't you play, too?" Jake turned and snared Rebecca in his arms.

"Jake, watch out. Your hands are still full of paint!" Rebecca's protest was ruined by her laughter. "And you've got a streak of yellow down your cheek."

"Oh, so now you're accusing me of being yellow, are you?" Jake growled. "You're gonna pay for that."

Rebecca shot a quick glance at Amy to make sure she wasn't frightened by their teasing struggle, but Amy was grinning at their antics.

Reassured, Rebecca dramatically declared, "Okay, you win! I surrender! Now let me go."

"Say the magic words first," he ordered.

"*Please* let me go."

"Uh-uh. Those aren't the magic words."

"Then what are they?"

"The magic words are 'Kiss me, Jake.'"

"Kiss me, Jake," she repeated in disbelief.

A second later he did.

Six

Rebecca's startled gasp reflected her astonishment as Jake's mouth claimed hers with surprising gentleness. His lips were warm, caring and so persuasive that she forgot they had an audience. Closing her eyes, Rebecca surrendered to the moment of magic. The kiss was now a gentle coupling, reflecting a mutual sense of expectancy.

To her surprise Jake didn't try increasing the intimacy of their embrace. He didn't take, he gave. His rare display of tenderness made her feel cherished, which in turn made her feel confused. If this was wrong, why did it feel so right?

Bill entered the kitchen in time to see his daughter reluctantly releasing herself from Jake's arms. Bill took the time to exchange a discreet thumbs-up sign with Dorothy before asking, "When's dinner? I'm starving."

"I seem to have developed quite an appetite myself," Jake announced with a slow smile in Rebecca's direction.

Before Rebecca could reply, Dorothy began issuing instructions to her and Jake, treating them as if they were Amy's age. "You two had better wash up before dinner. Now *both* of you have got a streak of yellow down your faces. And Amy's even got paint on her glasses!"

Feeling flustered, Rebecca checked Amy.

The little girl was frowning uncertainly. Amy wasn't used to seeing her mother in a man's arms, let alone being kissed.

Rebecca responded by kissing the top of Amy's head, one of the few places devoid of finger paint. "You look like a rainbow Popsicle," she whispered in her daughter's ear. "Maybe I should gobble you up!"

Amy giggled, and the tension passed.

"Dinner's in fifteen minutes," Dorothy announced, "so get a move on." She clapped her hands briskly. "I want to see everyone in the dining room."

Everyone complied, and for the first time since Jake had come to stay, Rebecca and Amy had dinner downstairs. The momentous occasion did not go unnoticed by her father and Jake. The congratulatory looks being exchanged between the two men prompted Rebecca into action. Jake and her father had had things their own way long enough. It was about time she tipped the scales a little more in her favor.

"All right, this is it!" she exclaimed after joining her father in the study later that evening. "I've decided to even the odds." She closed the door in the hope of ensuring some privacy. "While Dorothy's got Jake waylaid in the kitchen, I want you to tell me everything you know about him."

Bill looked up from the *Washington Post* he was reading, clearly surprised at her request.

"Come on," she prompted. "I'm sure you and Jake have already had a little chat about me. It's only fair that we have a little chat about him."

Putting his newspaper aside, Bill said, "I'd be delighted to talk about Jake. What would you like to know?"

"Everything." Rebecca sank into the maroon leather chair across from her father and made herself comfortable.

"Care to be more specific?"

"Has Jake ever discussed his background with you?"

"Not much."

"Fa-ther!"

Bill laughed at her plaintive exclamation. She hadn't sounded like that since he'd refused to let her drive the car on her sixteenth birthday. "Okay, okay. Take it easy. I'll tell you what I know, but as you may have noticed, Jake isn't exactly the talkative type—especially about himself. We've never really discussed his early years in any detail, but from the things he's mentioned in passing, I'd say that he grew up fairly quickly."

Jake managed to do a lot of things quickly, she thought to herself. Look how fast he'd moved in here. And after he had, it certainly hadn't taken him long to seriously threaten her well-built defenses. No doubt about it, Rebecca needed to know more about this man who was rapidly turning her life upside down.

"Jake was still with the police department when you first met him, wasn't he?" she asked her father.

Bill nodded.

"What was he like then?"

"Harder. Colder. Very remote. Not at all the way he is now."

Rebecca got a mental image of the cold stranger Jake had become when she'd told him she didn't want him to meet Amy. He'd become remote then, giving her a hint of what he must have been like when her father had first met him.

Bill's expression became troubled. "I remember him telling me at the time that he'd stopped caring, and that when you don't care there's not much difference between you and the people you're trying to put behind bars. That was right after he'd started taking my evening class. He looked like a man who'd been to hell and back."

"Old ghosts," she murmured softly.

"What?"

"Jake said something about coming back to Washington to exorcise old ghosts. Do you know what he meant by that?"

"Yes, I do, but I think Jake is the one who should tell you about it, not me."

"Are you sure Jake would be willing to talk about it?" she questioned hesitantly. "I don't want to reopen any old wounds that might be painful for him."

Bill was obviously pleased. "You care about him, don't you?"

Rebecca restlessly fidgeted with a brass bowl on the end table. "I've only known him a little more than a week."

"And?"

"And what?"

"And what do you think of him?"

"I wish I knew," she murmured.

"Well, you already know what I think of him," Bill said. "Jake is a good man with a strong sense of integrity. Did I happen to mention that he's insisted on paying for his keep while he's staying with us? I refused, told him he was an invited guest, but Jake was adamant. He said to put the money toward Amy's college fund, or a new boiler or whatever, but to keep the money. Said it was an order. And you know how Jake is about orders."

"Yes, he's very good at issuing orders."

"And you're not very good at obeying them," her father couldn't resist inserting. Anticipating her indignation, he lifted his hand in a conciliatory way. "I know, I know, you're a grown woman who can make her own decisions. I just hope you don't allow what's happened in the past, either yours or his, to cloud the issues in the present."

Her father's comments and actions had already made it clear that he thought Jake was right for her. There were even several times during the next week when Rebecca thought she might agree with her father. But then common sense would assert itself, and she would remind herself of the known facts. Jake's track record spoke for itself.

As for her new plan, she wasn't sure if fighting fire with fire was any more effective than running, but she had to admit that it was a lot more fun. The problem was that Jake was still making serious inroads to her heart. No other man had ever made her feel this way before, not even Ted. Thoughts of Jake distracted her at work and kept her awake at night. Whenever they were together, he had only to look at her and she felt weak all over.

Dorothy expressed similar symptoms, but her malady was diagnosed as the flu, and she was ordered to stay in bed. When her son insisted that she come stay with them out in Arlington, Dorothy was in no condition to argue.

"Don't worry about anything," Rebecca assured the housekeeper over the phone. "Everything here is under control."

It was only a slight fib, Rebecca assured herself after hanging up. Things weren't exactly out of control, at least not yet, but they soon would be unless a temporary schedule was set up. Reassigning Dorothy's work load was the first priority.

Rebecca took over the cooking, Bill took over the babysitting. Jake just took over in general. He also insisted on helping Rebecca clean up the kitchen after dinner.

But the haphazard way Jake was currently piling things into the dishwasher made Rebecca question the advisability of such a move. "Have you ever loaded a dishwasher before?"

He frowned. "What gave me away?"

The more
you love romance . . .
the more
you'll love this offer

FREE!

*Mail this
heart today!
(See inside)*

**Join us on a Silhouette® Honeymoon
and we'll give you
4 free books
A free manicure set
And a free mystery gift**

IT'S A
SILHOUETTE HONEYMOON —
A SWEETHEART
OF A FREE OFFER!

HERE'S WHAT YOU GET:

1. Four New Silhouette Desire® Novels — FREE!

Take a Silhouette Honeymoon with your four exciting romances — yours FREE from Silhouette Books. Each of these hot-off-the-press novels brings you the passion and tenderness of today's greatest love stories . . . your free passports to bright new worlds of love and foreign adventure.

2. A compact manicure set — FREE!

You'll love your beautiful manicure set — an elegant and useful accessory to carry in your handbag. Its rich burgundy case is a perfect expression of your style and good taste — and it's yours free with this offer!

3. An Exciting Mystery Bonus — FREE!

You'll be thrilled with this surprise gift. It will be the source of many compliments, as well as a useful and attractive addition to your home.

4. Money-Saving Home Delivery!

Join the Silhouette Desire subscriber service and enjoy the convenience of previewing 6 new books every month delivered right to your home. Each book is yours for only $2.24 — 26¢ less per book than what you pay in stores. And there is no extra charge for postage and handling. Great savings plus total convenience add up to a sweetheart of a deal for you!

5. Free Newsletter!

You'll get our monthly newsletter, packed with news on your favorite writers, upcoming books, even recipes from your favorite authors.

6. More Surprise Gifts!

Because our home subscribers are our most valued readers, we'll be sending you additional free gifts from time to time — as a token of our appreciation.

START YOUR SILHOUETTE HONEYMOON TODAY — JUST
COMPLETE, DETACH AND MAIL YOUR FREE-OFFER CARD

Get your fabulous gifts
ABSOLUTELY FREE!

MAIL THIS CARD TODAY.

GIVE YOUR HEART TO SILHOUETTE

Yes! Please send me my four Silhouette Desire novels FREE, along with my free manicure set and free mystery gift as explained on the opposite page.

PLACE HEART STICKER HERE

NAME _____
(PLEASE PRINT)

ADDRESS _____ APT. _____

CITY _____ STATE _____

ZIP CODE _____ 225 CIL JAYD

Prices subject to change. Offer limited to one per household and not valid to present subscribers.

SILHOUETTE BOOKS "NO-RISK" GUARANTEE

— There's no obligation to buy — and the free books and gifts remain yours to keep.

— You pay the lowest price possible and receive books before they appear in stores.

— You may end your subscription any time — just write and let us know.

PRINTED IN U.S.A.

START YOUR
SILHOUETTE HONEYMOON TODAY.
JUST COMPLETE, DETACH AND MAIL YOUR
FREE-OFFER CARD.

If offer card below is missing, write to:
Silhouette Books, 901 Fuhrmann Blvd., P.O. Box 9013, Buffalo, N.Y. 14240-9013

"A couple of things." She took a dirty plate out of his hand. "For one thing the food has to be scraped off the dishes before you put them in."

"What's the point of using a dishwasher if you have to clean the dishes first?"

"It's easier than doing all these dishes by hand."

"I use paper plates myself," he told her.

"Dorothy doesn't allow them in her kitchen."

"I won't tell if you won't," he suggested. "All right, stop looking so disapproving and tell me what else was wrong with my dish-loading technique."

She leaned over the dishwasher as she explained. "Plates go down here; glasses, cups and bowls up here."

Jake leaned right behind her, fitting her into the curve of his body. He wrapped her long hair around his left hand, moving it out of his way so he could nuzzle the back of her neck. His lips brushed her skin as he murmured, "How come?"

"Wh-what?" She couldn't think straight when he was this close.

"How come only plates go—" he slid his free hand down her thigh to her knee before pointing to the appliance's bottom rack "—down there?"

The man was incredible—even in a kitchen he devised ways to seduce her! She was tucked into his arms spoon fashion, and she could feel his lips softly nibbling on the ultrasensitive skin behind her ear—eroding her defenses and making her want him with an intensity that was almost painful. Now his hand returned to her knee, which he began lightly caressing through the gauzy cotton of her summer skirt.

"You never answered my question." His voice was dark and husky in her ear.

Rebecca had a few questions of her own. Where had he learned how to do that with his tongue, swirling it into her ear like that? The tiny caress gave her goose bumps. She shivered with pleasure. And where had he learned to do that with his fingers? She'd never known that the back of her knee was such an erogenous zone.

What had he asked her? she wondered hazily. Something about loading dishes? Her answer was unavoidably vague. "Umm, there's a . . . good reason."

"I suppose that means there's also a good reason why the other stuff goes up here?" he asked with pseudo-innocence while his hand slid up devilishly close to her breasts.

She grabbed his wrist before he took her breath, and her resistance, away. "There's also a good reason not to fool around in the kitchen." She turned in his arms and braced her hands on his chest. "My father or Amy could walk in here any minute."

Jake straightened but retained possession of her hands. "Don't you think Amy should get used to seeing me with you?"

"First let *me* get used to being with you," she suggested as she slipped out of his grasp and put the open dishwasher door between them. "You're rushing me again."

"No, I'm not. Making love to you on the kitchen table would be rushing you. This . . ." He reached over the half-filled dishwasher rack, took hold of her hand and kissed the inside of her wrist. "This is just fooling around. Why do I get the impression you haven't done much of it?"

His wry comment really dented her ego. Offended, she tried to tug her hand away.

He refused to let her go. "Now, don't go getting all huffy. I just meant that you seemed . . ."

"I seemed what?" she demanded defensively. "Rusty, out of practice?"

"Rusty, no. Nervous, yes. As for being out of practice, if that worries you, you've got my permission to practice on me anytime, any place. Feel free."

"It's not that easy for me," she muttered.

"It's not that easy for me, either, Rebecca." He released her hand and reached out to tip up her chin so that she was looking directly into his eyes. Then he gave her a sudden grin. "But, hey, if I can learn how to load a dishwasher, surely you can learn how to fool around in the kitchen."

His whimsical humor made her smile. "Especially since I have such a good teacher, right?"

He tried to look humble. "Modesty and good sense prevent me from answering that question."

With tongue in cheek, Rebecca reached for a linen dish towel, expertly twisted it into a long coiled rope and then cracked it like a whip—mockingly flicking it in Jake's direction. "Modesty, my foot!"

Her lighthearted response took him by surprise. So did the experienced way she handled that dish towel! But Jake was experienced, too, although not necessarily in the art of towel fighting. Grabbing the twisted end of the towel, he began a tug of war, which ended with his pulling her close enough to kiss her.

Rebecca had never had so much fun in the kitchen as she did during those next few days. Jake made the most tedious chores an adventure—even the laundry.

Thursday night was wash night, and Jake was supposedly helping her by folding the laundry. But what he was really doing was distracting her with his provocative comments.

"Just for future reference, I like this." He dangled her lavender-colored camisole from his index finger.

"I don't know, Jake. I think the color clashes with your eyes," she retorted.

"Funny, very funny," he growled. "Let's see how brave you are when you're not holding a basket full of laundry." Jake dropped the camisole and hauled the basket out of her arms. He then tugged her into his arms. "Now what do you have to say for yourself?"

"Plenty."

"That's what I was afraid of."

Leaning back in his arms, she studied his face. "I have a hard time imagining you being afraid of anything."

"When you're a cop, fear is something you learn to live with."

This was the first time he'd ever referred to his association with the police department, and she took advantage of the opening. "Is it something *you* learned to live with, Jake?"

"Yes."

"Does it bother you to talk about it?"

"No."

"Then why are you being so closemouthed?" she demanded in exasperation.

"Closemouthed? Me?" He leaned closer and brushed his parted lips across hers. After seducing the corner of her mouth with the tip of his tongue, he murmured, "Now, did that feel like I'm being closemouthed?"

Frustrated by his evasiveness, she freed herself from his embrace. "That's not what I meant, and you know it!"

Jake leaned one hip against the dryer and watched her make a hash out of folding one of Amy's little T-shirts. "Why don't you just come out and ask me what you want to know?" he suggested.

"Okay, I will." She tossed the T-shirt aside and turned to face him. "You once told me you'd come back to Washington to exorcise old ghosts. What did you mean by that?"

"You sure get right to the point, don't you?"

"I was merely following your orders."

"That'll be a first."

"You're avoiding my question."

"I'm trying to think of the right way to put this."

"Just tell me the truth, Jake. Did it have something to do with your police work?"

"I couldn't do my job effectively anymore," he said abruptly. Misinterpreting the confused look on her face, he added, "I wasn't dismissed or suspended, if that's what you're thinking. It was burnout. I'd been on the force for six years. That was long enough."

Long enough for what? Rebecca wondered. She got the distinct feeling there was more to the story than Jake was saying. She knew police work was a stressful occupation, but Jake was a strong and stubborn man. Something must have happened to trigger his burnout. Something must have happened to make him "stop caring," as her father had put it.

"And the old ghosts you referred to?" she asked him.

"My partner was killed in the line of duty."

Even though Jake's announcement was direct and unemotional, she saw the terrible pain reflected in his eyes. She wished she could say something to erase that look. "I'm sorry."

"Yeah, so was I. Sorry and out for revenge." His expression became grim as his mind flashed back to that time. Abe had been more than just his partner, he'd been Jake's best friend. He was a good man, the best; a loving husband to his wife Gloria, a fine father to his two small children. And he'd been shot down in the prime of his life. "I came real close...too close...to murdering the guy who killed Abe."

Jake looked so remote that Rebecca felt compelled to reach out and touch him. His arm was tense beneath her fingers, but gradually he relaxed and continued speaking.

"Anyway my reaction made me realize that it was time I got out. That's when I signed up for the writing course your father taught. Strangely enough, someone in the department recommended taking the writing class. He said it helped to get things straight in your head if you wrote them down. He was right.''

"So you quit your job in the police department to write full-time?''

"Hardly." He gave her a wry smile. "I still needed to eat, so I couldn't just up and quit. But I did begin moving away from that way of life. Spent all my spare time finishing my first book. Bill suggested having an agent read it. I got lucky. The agent accepted it and sold it to the second publisher he sent it to. Once that book sold I had enough to live on, what with the advance and the money I'd been saving. That's when I quit.''

"Did you always want to be a writer?''

Jake shrugged. "I never thought it was an obtainable goal until I took that course. What about you? Did you always want to be a cataloging librarian?''

She laughed and shook her head. "No way!''

"I didn't think so,'' he murmured. She was too full of life for such a quiet profession.

"I *really* wanted to be a children's librarian,'' she teased.

He tossed a folded pillow case at her. "You set me up on that one.''

"That'll teach you to stereotype librarians.''

"How about teaching me how to *seduce* a librarian. What do you say?''

"I only have one thing to say to you, Jake Fletcher.''

"Really? And what's that?''

"Kiss me.''

The words were barely spoken before Jake was complying with her unexpected but delightful request. He found her warm lips parted, ready to meet him halfway. She kissed him as he was kissing her—slowly, softly, passionately.

Hearing Jake's murmur of approval, Rebecca moved even closer. Her arms slid up his chest, over his shoulders and around his neck. From there her fingers were free to run through the sensuous thickness of his hair. It felt good. *He* felt good. And the way he was moving against her... felt... incredible. Her leg was wedged between his as he rocked his hips against her with gentle urgency.

Never in her entire life had Rebecca been more aware of, nor more grateful for, all the intimate differences between a man and a woman. Pleasure flooded through her. She and Jake fit so well together, like two halves of one whole. There was no mistaking the fact that he wanted her. Rebecca wanted him, too.

The signs of her own arousal were quickly becoming apparent to Jake. She didn't hide her hunger, neither did he. They were both consumed by the silent, seductive chant of *more, more*. Jake slid his hands beneath her knit top and caressed her. Rebecca reciprocated by unbuttoning his shirt so that she could touch him. From there things rapidly got out of hand. They were lost in the hot intimacies of seeking hands and sizzling kisses when a piercing buzzer went off right next to them. Startled, they broke apart.

The washing machine's timer was much easier to turn off than the intense passion they'd just aroused. The memory of the kisses they'd shared and the caresses they'd exchanged stayed with them both throughout that night.

The next morning Jake tried to get some writing done, but he couldn't keep his mind off Rebecca. Even his nifty briefcase-size word processor failed to inspire him. The text on the computer's small amber screen looked like a bunch of gibberish. Hoping that a break might improve his powers of concentration, Jake left his room and headed for the kitchen. Maybe a hefty dose of caffeine would do the trick.

The kitchen was already occupied. Amy was quietly playing with her stuffed toy, apparently trying to teach Pinkie how to use crayons. Bill, looking unusually harried, was pouring himself a cup of coffee from a fresh pot.

Jake sniffed appreciatively. "Ah, that must be what I smelled."

"I'm sorry, did I disturb you? I know how tough it is to be distracted when you're trying to get some writing done."

"No problem. I needed a break. I wasn't getting much accomplished anyway." Jake took a restorative gulp of the coffee he'd just poured for himself.

"If you're taking a break," Bill said hesitantly, "I wonder if I could ask a favor of you."

"Sure. What is it?"

"The dentist's office just called to tell me that they had a cancellation and can fit me in this afternoon. I've got a filling that's come loose. The problem is that Amy hates going to the dentist's office, even if she's not the patient. I wonder if you'd mind watching her while I go to my appointment."

"I don't mind if Amy doesn't mind."

"Amy, is it okay if Jake stays with you while Grandpa goes to the dentist?"

The little girl studied Jake for a moment before nodding. "Okay."

Bill sighed. "I'm glad that's settled. As it is, I won't even be able to do the grocery shopping I told Rebecca I'd do."

"I've got a solution for you. Amy and I can do the grocery shopping while you're at the dentist."

"That would be wonderful, Jake. Take my car. The dentist's office is only two blocks away, I can walk there."

"Where should I go to get the groceries?"

Bill pulled a sheet of paper out from under a magnetic apple stuck to the refrigerator door. "Rebecca wrote the directions on the back of the list."

After a twenty-minute drive, Jake finally pulled into the parking lot of the self-proclaimed SuperStore. Then he had to get Amy out of the car safety seat he'd had so much trouble getting her into. Putting her in the kiddie seat of the shopping cart wasn't any easier.

Jake thought it was silly to have a seat belt for a kid in a grocery cart, but that was before they got inside and he tried maneuvering through the aisles. Talk about congestion—the traffic was worse than rush hour on the Beltway. And since he was unfamiliar with the layout, his progress was slower than that of the experienced shoppers, who whizzed past him as if they were racing the Indy 500.

It took him five minutes to find the aisle for breakfast cereals, and when he got there, he discovered that aisle Ten was about as long as a football field. Attempting to find a box of ChocoWheats in the sea of cereal boxes was like looking for a needle in a haystack. After looking up and down the shelves several times, Jake finally had to enlist the assistance of a stock boy.

"Do you carry ChocoWheats?"

The stock boy didn't even look up from the box he was unpacking. "It's in with the breakfast cereal."

"Show me," Jake growled in a menacing voice that had always made even hardened criminals wince. It worked on the stock boy, who immediately rushed over and handed Jake a box.

"Thanks."

It was the same way in the tea aisle. Fifty kinds of tea, but nothing called Sweet Slumber Chamomile. Another stock boy was called over.

At this rate it'll take me three days to get through this list, Jake thought to himself in disgust. There had to be an easier way.

It certainly wasn't to be found in the paper goods aisle. Oh, he found the proper brand of toilet paper easily enough, even the right color, but when he grabbed it, he barely prevented a towering pyramid of toilet paper rolls from tumbling down around him.

Amy was impressed. "More, more!"

Two aisles over he wasn't as successful at preventing several boxes of baking soda from falling off the top shelf after he reached for one. They might call this place a SuperStore, but there was nothing super about shopping in it, Jake decided as he stifled a curse. You were lucky to get out in one piece. And then you had to worry about where to put everything. Did six bags of groceries fit into a Triumph Spitfire?

Not very easily, he soon discovered. "Where does Dorothy put all the groceries when she comes here?" he muttered.

Amy answered the question for him. "Dotty drives her car. The big one."

Jake didn't even know that Dorothy had a car. So much for his powers of observation.

"You sent him where?" Rebecca asked after finding that her father was the only one home.

"Grocery shopping."

"At the SuperStore?"

Bill nodded.

"It's the Friday before the Memorial Day weekend. The place will be packed. He took Amy with him?"

"She wanted to go."

"When did they leave?"

"Not long ago."

"How long?"

"A few hours."

"How few?"

"Three," Bill admitted.

"They should have been back ages ago. What could be taking them so long?"

"Wait, I think that's them now. Yes, it is. See? I told you there was nothing to worry about."

What Rebecca saw was Jake's swollen lip. "What happened? Were you in a fight?"

"I had a disagreement with a box of baking soda. Now I know why it says Arm and Hammer," he said ruefully.

"What happened?"

"I didn't duck in time."

"Mommy, I had fun," Amy announced. "Look, I got a sticker! Pinkie got one, too!" Amy showed Rebecca the red circle stuck to her hand.

"The cashier put one on Amy and one on the gallon of milk. They should have given me a sticker, too—for valor," Jake decided as he set two bags on the kitchen counter. "I had no idea doing the family grocery shopping was such a dangerous occupation." He gingerly ran a finger across his swollen lip. "The merchandise doesn't attack you at a Seven-Eleven. You just run in, pick up your stuff, pay for it and leave. No big deal."

Rebecca stepped over to the sink and ran cold water on a paper towel. "Come here and I'll fix you up."

"That sounds kind of kinky to me," Jake murmured.

"What's kinky mean, Mommy?" Amy asked.

"He said Pinkie, not kinky," Rebecca hastily interceded. "Now be quiet, Jake, while I patch you up." She gave him a quelling look.

"Mommy, wanna Smurf Band-Aid?" Amy asked.

"No, I don't think he'll need one. Thanks anyway, Amy. Why don't you go see what Grandpa wants for dinner."

"Sorry about that," Jake said after Amy had gone. "I'm still new at this kid stuff."

"Have you gotten your fill of family life yet?" Rebecca inquired ruefully.

Jake shook his head. "I'm not a man who gives up easily."

Rebecca was beginning to believe that. She was beginning to believe *him*.

Seven

"I can't believe you lived in Washington for six years and never made it to the zoo, Jake," Rebecca said as she and Amy stood in line with him outside the National Zoo the next day.

"I can't believe you've been back six months and haven't brought Amy here before," he retorted. "She's a kid, and zoos were meant for kids."

The spur-of-the-moment excursion had been Jake's idea, and it was hard to tell who was more excited, he or Amy. Watching him talk to Amy, Rebecca realized how well her daughter and Jake were getting along. That grocery shopping excursion the two of them had shared yesterday seemed to have forged a new bond between them. As Jake frequently reminded her, he was still new at all this kid stuff, but he was doing exceptionally well for a beginner.

A tug on her hand brought her attention back to Amy.

She was pointing to a balloon vendor who'd wisely set up shop right outside the zoo's Connecticut Avenue entrance.

Noting Amy's interest, Jake asked, "Would you like one of those balloons?"

Amy looked at her mother for approval before nodding shyly.

"What color do you want?"

Jake had to crouch down to hear her answer. "Pink."

"How about you, Rebecca? What color do you want?"

Her first thought was how sexy he made *Rebecca* sound. He hadn't spoken her name very often, but each time he did she melted a little inside. She hugged the feeling to herself even as she denied needing a balloon.

Jake bought her one anyway. "Here you go, a pink one for Amy..." He carefully handed it to the little girl. "And a red one for Rebecca." He presented a metallic heart-shaped balloon to Rebecca with a special flourish. Taking her hand he wrapped her fingers around the string and then wrapped his fingers around hers. "Take care of that. I wouldn't want you breaking it."

The look he gave her made her feel as if he really was entrusting her with his heart. The surrounding crowd faded away. Even though their only physical contact was their entwined fingers, Rebecca felt as if he'd touched her intimately. Her heart was beating like a wild thing, her breathing uneven. A primitive need throbbed deep within her. He was speaking to her with his eyes, promising her wicked pleasures and sensuous excitement.

In that moment both Jake and Rebecca forgot their master plans. It was no longer possible to separate themselves from what was happening to them. This magic they shared was growing more powerful every day until it was bigger than the two of them, bigger than their objections. It was all-consuming. But was it love? Or merely passion? Such important questions, but neither one of them had the answers.

The sound of Amy's cry cut into their thoughts.

"My balloon!" Amy wailed as it wafted up into the sky.

"That's okay, I'll get you another one," Jake promised her.

"And this time we'll tie the balloon to Pinkie so it doesn't get away," Rebecca added.

Once that was accomplished and they were actually inside the zoo, Rebecca said, "I think our first order of business should be getting a stroller for Amy before they run out of them."

Amy had refused to use the stroller they had at home, insisting she was a big girl and the dumb stroller was for babies. Although shy, Amy could be very stubborn. Luckily she was so enthralled with her first trip to the zoo that she didn't complain about having to sit in one of the zoo's strollers. Apparently she didn't think it was "dumb." She just wanted it to move faster.

"Look, Mommy! Look!" Amy got so excited that her glasses almost slid off her nose. "Bambi!" She leaned forward in the stroller. "Hurry! Hurry!"

"Maybe you'd better let me handle the stroller," Jake suggested. "After the training I had with that shopping cart yesterday, I'm getting to be a real pro."

Rebecca stepped aside to allow Jake to take her place behind the stroller.

"No, don't go too far away. In fact, just to be on the safe side, you'd better keep one hand on the push bar here, just in case I do something wrong."

He wasn't doing a damn thing wrong, and he knew it! Rebecca thought to herself. He was doing everything just right, touching her, looking at her, making her want him. It didn't help matters any that once they reached the deer enclosures, Amy didn't want to move. Now that Jake didn't have to concentrate on steering the stroller, he was free to continue his seduction. Lifting their entwined hands, he nibbled on Rebecca's fingers.

"The animals are getting hungry," he murmured.

So am I, she thought to herself with a hint of desperation. She had to get this caravan moving again before she melted on the spot.

"Come on, let's look for the panthers like Pinkie," Rebecca suggested, knowing full well that the large cats were at the other end of the zoo.

Amy soon forgot her enchantment with the deer as they came upon the impressive Great Flight Cage. She was clearly intrigued by the strange-looking structure. "What's that?"

"That's a special place for birds," Rebecca answered. "It's built in that funny tent shape so the birds have lots of room to fly around, and it's covered with special mesh so they don't fly away."

They went on to visit the new Smokey the Bear and the famous Chinese giant pandas. Amy was disappointed in the pandas, who were sleeping, but she was fascinated by the giraffes.

After taking a ride on the zoo's tram, they ended up at the picnic area on the other side of the zoo. There they found a bench and ate hot dogs purchased from a vendor. The food was hardly gourmet fare—the french fries were limp and lukewarm, but Rebecca had never enjoyed a meal more.

Jake appeared to be enjoying himself, too. He looked great. It was a warm day so he'd rolled up the sleeves of his pale blue chambray shirt. His arms were tanned and muscular. The jeans he wore had been washed so many times that they'd achieved a priceless fit. The way they emphasized the lean lines of his body had caused appreciative looks from a number of women.

One woman in particular was staring at Jake—and had been for some time now. She looked to be in her late fifties and was accompanied by a man whom Rebecca presumed to be her husband.

"Do you know that woman over there?" Rebecca asked Jake.

"Which woman where?"

Rebecca discreetly tilted her head in the woman's direction. "The one who's walking this way."

"I don't recognize her," he replied.

But the woman had recognized Jake. "Excuse me, I hate to bother you, but aren't you Jake Fletcher, the author of *Vengeance*?"

Jake nodded.

"I just loved your book!" the woman enthused. "I own a bookstore here in town, and I specialize in suspense. Both of your books have done really well in my store. I told my husband that I thought it was you, but he didn't believe me. Milt, it is him!" she yelled over to her husband triumphantly. "I told you so!" Obviously the gregarious sort, the woman turned her attention to Amy. "And who's this?" she exclaimed, looking from Jake to Amy, trying to find a family resemblance. "Your little girl?"

Rebecca attributed Jake's strange expression to discomfort at being recognized. Meanwhile, Amy was nervously shifting even closer to Rebecca, who smiled reassuringly and put an arm around her. "We're just friends of Jake's," Rebecca finally answered on his behalf.

"I wonder if I could have an autograph, Mr. Fletcher?" the woman requested. "I want to display it in my store to prove that I really met you—right here at the zoo. Nobody would believe me otherwise."

Jake obligingly signed his name to the sheet of paper she handed him.

"Thanks so much, and good luck with your next book."

"You okay?" Rebecca asked him after the woman had left. "You seem kind of preoccupied."

"I'm fine. Just surprised, that's all."

She assumed he was referring to being asked for his autograph. "Just wait until your books come out in paperback," she said. "Even more people will recognize you then. You'll get used to it."

Being recognized was the last thing on Jake's mind. What really had thrown him was his reaction to the simple question about Amy being his little girl. He'd wanted to say yes, that she was his.

It was the first time Jake had ever felt possessive about Amy. Oh, he'd been feeling possessive about Rebecca practically from the first minute he'd laid eyes on her—but this paternal feeling toward Amy was new to him. He'd always thought of her as "Rebecca's kid," but he was discovering that Amy was more than just part of a package deal. He was beginning to realize that she was someone special in her own right.

"Mommy, where's the am...aminals like Pinkie?" Amy asked.

"The *animals* like Pinkie are in the Lion House. Are you done with that hot dog?"

Amy nodded.

"Okay." Rebecca wiped the ketchup off the little girl's chin. Amy looked so sweet in her pink sun hat, flowered top and pink pants. After nudging her daughter's glasses back into place, Rebecca kissed her nose. "First we'll take a bathroom stop, and then we're off to see the Lion House."

They not only saw the Lion House, but also the Monkey House. They skipped the Reptile House, at Rebecca's request—creepy-crawlies had never been her favorites.

Rebecca's feet were aching by the time they took another rest stop to enjoy a snack. While Jake ordered an ice cream cone for Amy, Rebecca opted for a cold can of soda. They were lucky enough to find an empty bench.

It felt so good to sit down. The outfit she was wearing, navy cotton slacks and a red camp shirt, was perfect for the day's outing, but her shoes left something to be desired. As unobtrusively as possible, Rebecca slid her foot out of her sandal and placed the cold side of her soda can against the hot sole of her foot. She sighed. Ah, relief.

Jake was watching her performance with heated interest. Her face displayed such sensuous satisfaction that he couldn't help fantasizing about taking her to bed. Would she tilt her head back and smile like that when he made her his? Would she sigh or moan?

As if hearing his thoughts, Rebecca opened her eyes and looked at Jake. The heat of the midday sun was nothing compared to the searing intensity of his stare. He was eyeing her the way a hungry lion eyes fresh meat.

Amy sat between them, unaware of the silently evocative exchange between her mother and Jake. Amy was much more concerned with her ice cream, which was melting faster than she could eat it. Trying to hurry, the little girl took a giant lick. Unfortunately the lopsided scoop of ice cream toppled off the cone and plopped right into Jake's lap.

"Uh-oh." Amy said in a little voice.

With an efficiency born of three-plus years of experience, Rebecca hurriedly took a handful of paper napkins and reached across Amy to scoop the ice cream off Jake's lap before it could do much damage.

The feel of her hands on that most sensitive part of his anatomy almost drove Jake over the edge. His blood burned, and his arousal was obvious as Rebecca dabbed at the stain.

"This should only take a minute," she said in a strangled voice.

Jake closed his eyes. "Ah, honey, take as long as you want."

Want. Oh, she wanted all right. She wanted to explore him and have him explore her. She wanted him in all the intimate ways a woman wants a man—taking him in her hands and guiding him into her body. She wanted to feel him moving, arousing, satisfying this awful hunger within her. Rebecca's face burned. She'd never had such nakedly erotic thoughts before.

"You'd better take care of the rest yourself," she muttered.

"You're the only one who can take care of what's wrong with me," Jake muttered in return. But he did take the napkins and complete the cleanup operation himself.

For the next half hour Rebecca and Jake avoided touching each other. Both needed the time to recover.

They ran into another unexpected bout of trouble when Amy saw her first walrus and began shrieking, "Monsters, monsters!"

Rebecca tried reassuring her. "Honey, that's a walrus, not a monster. It's just an animal, nothing to be afraid of."

But Amy refused to be placated and didn't settle down until they left that area of the zoo. By then the long day was catching up with the little girl, and she soon drifted off to sleep in the stroller.

"Do you think she was talking about the monsters you told me she dreams about?" Jake quietly asked Rebecca.

She nodded.

"How long has she been having these nightmares?"

"Almost a year. They began while we were still in Chicago."

"Is it always the same dream?"

"I'm not sure. I can't get her to talk about it. She wakes up crying and screaming about monsters, but that's all she'll say."

Jake knew how it felt to fight demons while sleeping. After Abe's death he'd had his share of nightmares. Sometimes he still got them, waking up in a cold sweat in the middle of the night. It was hard enough dealing with it as an adult; he could imagine how terrifying nightmares must be for a kid.

Amy seemed to be sleeping quietly now. In fact, she was dead to the world. She didn't even wake up when Rebecca scooped her out of the stroller and into her arms.

"That probably wasn't very good planning on my part," Rebecca murmured after Jake had returned the stroller.

"What wasn't?" he asked.

"I meant to stop at the washroom before turning the stroller back in. Well, it's not a big problem. Here, you hold Amy." Rebecca put her still-sleeping daughter in his arms. "I won't be long."

Jake panicked. "Rebecca, wait," he said in a desperate voice. "I don't know how to hold a kid!"

"Carefully, that's how. And quietly, so she doesn't wake up. Don't worry, I'll be right back."

Between holding Amy and hanging on to Pinkie, complete with deflated pink balloon, Jake had his hands full. Amy was still out like a light, her cheek resting against his shoulder. It felt strange having such a little bundle of warmth in his arms. He felt that strange tug at his heart again, only this time he couldn't attribute it to a pastrami on rye.

Amy shifted in her sleep, and Jake almost had a heart attack. He had one hand under her bottom and the other behind her back. Was he holding her right? Sure he'd picked her up to put her in the shopping cart and the car seat yesterday, but he hadn't had to hang on to her like this. What if he dropped her? What if he hurt her by holding her too tightly?

She sure was a little thing. A real flyweight. He hoisted her a little higher, so that her dangling foot no longer threatened to emasculate him. One kick from that little

Minnie Mouse gym shoe and he'd have been walking funny for a week. Having already had ice cream dumped on his lap, Jake was wary of any more unexpected pitfalls. He'd faced shoot-outs without flinching, and yet here he was, a nervous wreck over holding a little kid.

If any of the guys from the old precinct could have seen him now, they wouldn't have believed their eyes. Jake, the Lone Wolf, carrying a kid and a stuffed toy? No way. None of his readers would have believed it either. Would Mike Hammer change diapers? Would James Bond wipe away a three-year-old's tears? Not likely.

But these were things Jake found that he wanted to experience. He wondered if Rebecca wanted more kids, and then he wondered what it would be like sharing a child with Rebecca. A little girl like Amy, or a little boy he could teach how to play baseball.

Rebecca returned to find Jake looking down at Amy with the strangest look on his face. It was wistful and almost tender. She would've given a lot to know what he was thinking. Had he found today's taste of parenthood to his liking? For not having had any experience with children, he was certainly coping very well.

Still, he did look a little relieved to hand Amy back to her. Rebecca didn't hold it against him. She could still remember how frightening it was to hold a child for the first time.

"See, that wasn't so difficult, was it?" she said softly.

"Piece of cake," he confirmed with jaunty confidence.

"Let's sit down a minute so I can get organized. We seem to be leaving the zoo with twice as much stuff as we came in with. I don't think it will all fit back in here." She tried stuffing Pinkie into the carryall, but there was no room left. "This is an unexplained phenomenon that always seems to occur whenever I pack anything."

The sound of Jake's laughter wasn't loud enough to wake Amy, who was sleeping on Rebecca's lap, but it was enough to catch Rebecca's attention. His exceptionally good mood surprised her. "You really seem to be enjoying yourself today," she noted.

"You sound surprised."

"I am," she admitted. "I didn't think you'd get so much fun out of something as mundane as a trip to the zoo. It's not exactly life in the fast lane."

"What makes you think I have such a craving for the fast life?" he demanded. His voice held equal parts of exasperation and irritation. "Six years on the police force were enough to rid me of any hankering for excitement I might have had. I'm tired of moving on."

Rebecca was afraid to believe his words, so she hid her real feelings beneath a layer of mockery. "You mean the rolling stone is actually considering putting down roots?"

"You know, he must really have done quite a job on you."

His non sequitur completely confused her. "What are you talking about?"

"The man who made you so suspicious. The man who made you so cautious, the one who hurt you. Was it your husband?"

She nodded slowly.

"I thought it might have been." Correctly reading her thoughts, he said, "No, your father didn't tell me anything. You've given me plenty of clues yourself, including the fact that you've reverted to using your maiden name."

"That doesn't necessarily mean anything, Jake."

"I think it does. Why don't you tell me about it."

Rebecca looked back on that period as one of the lowest points of her life. Even after two years, it was still hard for her to talk about. She spoke slowly and reluctantly. "I married Ted less than a month after meeting him. I blindly ignored our differences. Family is important to me. It wasn't to him. I didn't know that then; I didn't know *him* then. I'm not making that mistake again."

"I'm not going to hurt you, Rebecca. Trust me."

"Trust takes time. Please, don't rush me. Give me time to believe you."

Jake studied her face for several moments before conceding. "I'll give you time if you'll give me something."

"What?" She couldn't help it, her voice and her expression were both wary.

Her distrust made him mutter under his breath. "Stop being so suspicious, and give me an honest chance. Don't judge me by your former husband's actions. Ghosts from the past are damn hard to fight. Agreed?"

Rebecca nodded. He was right. "Agreed."

"Good." He dropped a quick kiss to the tip of her nose. "Listen, how about going to the tidal basin tomorrow? I've always wanted to rent one of those paddleboats. What do you think?"

Before she could answer, someone bellowed, "Hey, Fletcher! Is that you?"

Unable to pinpoint where the shout had come from, Rebecca said, "Another one of your admiring fans?"

Jake shook his head. "A fellow police officer. Excuse me a minute."

Jake reached Patrolman Larry Henderson before he reached them.

"I didn't know you were back in town." Larry Henderson pumped Jake's hand in a bone-crushing handshake. "The famous writer comes home, huh? Sure beats being a cop. Pays better, too, I'll bet. You a millionaire yet? No? What are you doing here? The zoo doesn't seem like your kind of place."

That was the second time someone had said that about him, and Jake was getting tired of hearing it. His irritation was apparent. "What does anybody do at the zoo? I'm looking at the animals."

"Hey, right, you always did have a way with animals, Fletcher."

Larry laughed in a way Jake didn't appreciate. Now Jake remembered why he'd never liked the guy.

"You here alone?" Larry asked.

"No, I'm here with a friend."

"A lady friend, I'll bet. You always were great with women. Hey, that's not the lady, is it? The one sitting over there holding the kid?"

"Something wrong with that?"

"No, nothing," Larry hastily reassured a dangerous-looking Jake. "I just never figured you to be the family type. Wait till the guys hear this. They won't believe it. Jake Fletcher. At the zoo. With a kid, no less. I tell you, they won't believe it."

Larry walked away still shaking his head in disbelief.

Jake walked away determined to prove to Rebecca, to Larry, to the world that he was more than capable of being a family man.

"Everything okay?" Rebecca asked when Jake rejoined them.

"Everything's fine."

Despite his reassurance, Rebecca sensed that something *was* wrong. She wondered why Jake hadn't introduced them to his friend but felt awkward asking.

Jake followed her train of thought. "I would have introduced you, but I didn't know the guy that well, and I didn't want to wake Amy. Here, I'll carry her for you. Come on, let's go home."

Jake was unusually quiet during the cab ride back to Georgetown, and Rebecca was worried about his silence. Amy slept all the way home, only waking up as they entered the front door.

"Where's Pinkie?" was her first question.

Rebecca and Jake looked at each other in dismay. The cab! Pinkie had somehow gotten left behind in the cab.

They immediately called the cab company, to no avail. By the time the dispatcher located and radioed the driver, the stuffed toy was long gone.

Amy was desolate. She cried her heart out.

Muttering something about having things to do, Jake made a hasty getaway. *When the going gets tough, the tough get going,* Rebecca thought to herself. Amy continued crying. Nothing Rebecca or Bill said made any difference. Even a phone call from Dorothy didn't cheer her up.

"I want Pinkie!" she wailed.

Rebecca was about ready to cry herself after several hours of unsuccessful attempts to stop Amy's tears.

Jake didn't return until after dark. Rebecca had a glass of wine in her hand when she answered his quiet knock on her apartment door.

"Where's Amy?" he asked.

"In bed," Rebecca said curtly. As far as she was concerned Jake had abandoned ship.

"I've got something for her," Jake announced triumphantly. Like a magician pulling a white rabbit out of a hat, he pulled a stuffed Pink Panther toy out of a bag. "I bought her a new one."

His gesture surprised and touched her. "Was that where you've been all this time?"

Jake nodded. "I had no idea it would be so hard to find one."

"That was really sweet of you, Jake, but I don't think it will help." Rebecca sighed wearily. "Amy wants *her* Pinkie, not a new Pink Panther stuffed animal."

He wriggled the stuffed animal in front of her. "But this one's just like Pinkie."

"No, but it could be." Her expression became thoughtful. She took the toy from him.

"What are you doing?" Jake demanded in horror as she began twisting the Pink Panther's ear until it ripped.

"I'm fixing it so that it looks like Pinkie. Otherwise she'd know the difference. Pinkie had a ripped right ear and even though he'd been washed numerous times, there was still a fruit punch stain on his front here. I suppose if I dabbed some fruit punch there..."

"Hold on!" Jake grabbed the stuffed animal away from her. "You're not putting fruit punch on this thing. Do you know how many stores I had to go to before I found it? There's no way I'm going to let you ruin it."

"I'm not going to ruin it," she denied. "I'm going to fix it so that it looks like Pinkie."

"Why?"

"Because giving Amy her original Pinkie, or what she *thinks* is the original Pinkie, is the only thing that will make her feel better. I'm telling you, Jake, I know what I'm doing."

Their discussion was cut short by the sound of a child's terrified scream. Amy was having another nightmare.

Eight

―――

The sound of Amy's scream unsettled Jake and sent Rebecca rushing down the hall to her daughter's side.

"It's okay, honey." Rebecca sat on the little girl's bed and gathered her in her arms. "Mommy's right here. There's nothing to be scared of."

"Mmm . . . monsters!" Amy stuttered in between sobs.

"There aren't any monsters here," Rebecca reassured her. "It was just a bad dream."

Amy shook her head and stuck by her story. "Monsters . . . in the closet!"

"There are no monsters in the closet, Amy. Look, I'll show you." Rebecca was all set to get up, but Amy refused to let her go.

"No! No!" she kept crying.

Rebecca tried using logic. "Amy, why do you think there are monsters in the closet?"

"I saw them."

"But you were just dreaming, honey. Dreams aren't real. You didn't really see any monsters. And if you'd let go of me for a second, I'll show you that there's nothing in your closet except your clothes and toys. No monsters."

But no amount of cajoling could convince Amy to either loosen her hold on Rebecca or to stop crying.

Out in the living room, Jake was frantically pacing back and forth, longing for a shot of whiskey to settle his nerves. The little girl's scream had scared the hell out of him. And now her crying had him racked with guilt. He wasn't even sure why he felt guilty. Maybe it was for forgetting Pinkie in that damn cab. Or maybe it was for not knowing how to get rid of a little girl's nightmares. A real family man would know what to do.

Not that Rebecca seemed to be having any better luck, Jake realized. She'd been in there almost fifteen minutes, and Amy was still crying.

Jake's concern finally got the best of him. Following the sound of Amy's crying, he located her bedroom. As he stood out in the hallway, Jake was abruptly plagued by that old childhood feeling of being an outsider. But then Rebecca looked up and, seeing him, smiled with relief. In an instant Jake's feeling of cold isolation disappeared and was replaced with the warmth of belonging. He came closer.

The pink and white room was illuminated by a white lamp shaped like a sleeping cat. Amy's face was dripping with tears. Without her glasses she looked so defenseless.

"What's wrong?" he asked.

"Amy's convinced that there are monsters in the closet." The slight break in Rebecca's voice revealed the fact that she was nearly at the end of her rope.

"Monsters, huh?" Jake rubbed his chin and thought for a moment before suggesting, "Maybe I should just march those monsters out of the closet and tell them to stop bothering you."

Rebecca's protest of "Jake!" was drowned out by the sound of Amy's tremulous question. "Can you really make the monsters go away?" she asked Jake.

"Sure I can. Didn't your grandpa ever tell you that I was a cop, uh . . . I mean that I was a policeman once? And all policemen know how to get rid of monsters."

"Do you shoot them?" Amy asked with fear in her eyes.

"No, I don't shoot them. I just lead them out of the house."

Amy seemed to like that idea. "Do they come back?"

"I've never had any monsters come back, but if they should, I'd just lead them right out again. No big deal. Do you want to put your glasses on and watch?"

Jake's calm, no-nonsense approach toward dealing with monsters eased Amy's fears. It also left Rebecca wondering why she hadn't come up with that idea herself, instead of spending all these months telling Amy the monsters weren't real. They were obviously very real to Amy, and handling them accordingly was a brilliant move.

How had Jake known? Rebecca wondered as he opened the closet door and proceeded to lead Amy's monsters out of the room. Was it because he'd had to deal with so many monsters of his own? Whatever his reasoning, his actions were very successful. Amy immediately settled down. After insisting that Jake read her a short bedtime story she even fell asleep again.

"Thanks for your help," Rebecca whispered out in the hallway.

Jake held his finger up to his lips. "Shhh." He indicated that they should return to the living room by pointing his thumb in that direction.

Rebecca nodded her agreement. A few seconds later she gratefully sank onto the couch. Jake sat next to her.

"That was a wonderful idea," she quietly congratulated him.

"I wasn't sure it would work," Jake confessed. "I'm just glad it did."

"So am I." Rebecca silently acknowledged the fact that Jake hadn't just taken care of her daughter's monsters tonight, he'd also taken care of a lot of her own demons as well. He'd proved how good he was with Amy. But would Jake still be around to take care of Amy's monsters if they came back again, say in a month, or in a year? What were his plans for the future? He said he wanted to settle down, that he was ready for roots. But he'd said that before he'd really experienced family life. Even now, all of this was still new and challenging to him. Only time would tell how Jake would feel once the novelty wore off.

Right now Rebecca only knew that the more time she spent with Jake, the more time she wanted to spend with him. And the more she just plain wanted him—period!

"Are you planning on throwing that thing at me?" he inquired.

"What?" Belatedly, Rebecca realized that she was nervously twisting the newly purchased stuffed animal in her hands. "No, of course not. I was just thinking."

"About what?"

His question made her feel absurdly flustered. "About how I'm going to turn this guy into Pinkie so I can give him to Amy first thing in the morning," she fabricated. Latching onto her duties as a hostess, she asked, "Would you like a drink?"

Jake shook his head and gently removed the mangled toy from her hands. "I'd like you to have dinner with me."

"I already ate dinner tonight, but I can fix something for you if you're hungry." She bounced up from the couch.

Jake tugged her right back down. "Oh, I'm hungry all right, but not for food." Hooking a finger under her chin, he tipped up her face. When her eyes met his he said, "I wasn't trying to cadge a meal."

"What were you trying to do?"

"Ask you out on a date." He gave her a rueful smile. "I think it's about time, don't you?"

She returned his smile. "When?"

"Friday night. That will give you all week to get used to the idea."

She nodded. "Okay."

He nodded, too. "Okay."

The words were meaningless. The real communication was visual, not verbal, as they both shared the same thoughts, the same fantasies.

I want you.

I want you, too.

When?

Soon, soon.

"Whatcha doin', Mommy?" Amy asked as Rebecca stood in front of the bathroom mirror on Friday evening, carefully trying to apply eyeliner.

"I'm putting on makeup."

"Can Pinkie have some makeup, too?" Amy set her stuffed animal on the bathroom counter, happily unaware that this Pinkie was actually an imposter.

"No." Rebecca took a tube of lipstick out of Amy's eager hands. "Only Mommy can wear makeup."

"How come?"

"Because."

"Trixie wears makeup," Amy triumphantly informed her.

Rebecca ignored the reference to Amy's invisible friend. "I thought you were supposed to be getting ready for bed."

"Trixie gets to stay up late."

Rebecca decided that some child psychology was called for here. "Amy doesn't get to stay up late, but she does get to hear a bedtime story if she gets ready for bed like a good girl."

"Goodie! I want the zoo story. Can Jake read me the zoo story? He makes neat am—" Amy paused and corrected herself "—an...i...mal noises."

Remembering Jake's animal impersonations from their visit to the zoo, Rebecca smiled. "Okay, I'll ask Jake to read you the zoo story, but only if you hurry and get your jammies on before he comes. Now scoot."

With Pinkie stuffed under her arm, Amy scurried out of the bathroom and across the hall to her own bedroom.

Rebecca capped the eyeliner pencil and leaned forward to check her appearance in the mirror. The black dress she was wearing was the same one she'd worn when she'd first encountered Jake in that elevator. It was the most elegant outfit she owned. She wished she had the money to buy something else. He'd already seen her in this. Granted the woven gold belt was a new addition, but it still looked too...familiar. She didn't want to look familiar, she wanted to look glamorous. But glamorous was beyond her limited budget. Familiar would have to do.

Maybe if she piled her newly washed and curled hair up on top of her head and artistically arranged a few wispy tendrils in strategic locations... Ten minutes later Rebecca nodded approvingly. That looked better. Add a pair of dangling gold earrings, lacy black stockings, strappy black heels, and voilà—instant sophistication. Or so she hoped.

It was precisely seven o'clock when Jake came calling. As soon as she opened the door, Rebecca knew he recognized the dress. She'd expected that he would. But she hadn't expected the gleam of approval she saw in his dark eyes. He didn't say anything; he really didn't have to. The way he was looking at her said plenty. But it was still nice to hear the words.

"Well?" she prompted. "Is this okay?"

He slowly shook his head. "No, it's not okay. It's much better than just okay. It's beautiful, and so are you."

"Thank you."

"You're welcome," he said with a solemn courtesy that was in direct contrast to the devilishly naughty look he was giving her.

"Mommy, I'm in bed now!" Amy yelled down the hall.

"She's waiting for you to read her a bedtime story," Rebecca told Jake. "Do you mind?"

"Hey, I'm a born storyteller, remember?"

Rebecca remembered everything about Jake—every look, every kiss, every embrace. There hadn't been many kisses or embraces this past week, however. In fact, she and Jake hadn't gotten the chance to spend much time together at all. Things seemed to be conspiring against them. Dorothy was back, so there were no more chances for a romantic rendezvous by the dishwasher or an embrace in the laundry room. But tonight she hoped they'd be able to make up for lost time.

Jake was hoping the same thing while reading Amy a condensed version of her bedtime story. When Amy interrupted him in the middle of his bearlike growl he was afraid that she'd noticed that he'd skipped over several pages. She probably had this zoo story memorized.

Leaning forward with secretive confidentiality, Amy whispered, "You know what?"

He was almost afraid to ask, but he did. "No, what?"

"I think my mommy likes you."

Jake grinned. "You think so?"

Amy nodded and rolled her eyes. "She even put on makeup!"

Jake looked suitably impressed. "She did?"

"Uh-huh."

"Wow!" As he said it, Jake realized that he hadn't used that word since he was a kid himself, but somehow it seemed appropriate under the circumstances.

"What are you two whispering about in here?" Rebecca inquired from the doorway.

"It's a secret," Amy said.

Rebecca caught the shared looks between Jake and Amy as they sat there with their heads so close together. It was a moment Rebecca wanted to freeze in time and hold in her memory forever. The tough loner and the shy little girl, exchanging confidences—both grinning like a pair of Cheshire cats.

"Secrets, huh?" Rebecca came closer. "Well, I'll tell you my secret." She smoothed the rumpled covers and tucked Amy in. "It's time for lights out."

Amy immediately complained. "My story's not done yet, Mommy."

"I'll read it to you," Dorothy offered as she joined them. "The front door was open, so I came on in," the housekeeper added for Rebecca's benefit.

"Can you growl like a bear, Dottie?" Amy asked her.

"Sure can, and I can squeal like an eel, too," Dorothy bragged before turning her attention back to Jake and Rebecca. "Time for you two to make your exit."

"I left the name and number of the restaurant next to the phone," Rebecca told the housekeeper.

"Would you stop being such a worrywart? Your father and I will take good care of Amy. Forget about us for a while. Take her out and show her a good time," Dorothy gruffly instructed Jake, who mockingly tipped his head and said "Yes, ma'am."

Jake did show her a good time, and he began by taking her to an expensive restaurant that specialized in soft lighting and quiet intimacy along with delicious food. The entrées listed on the menu were all so tempting that Rebecca didn't know which one to choose. She finally decided on the sautéed crabmeat. Jake chose the filet mignon.

"So you approve of the place?" Jake asked her after their order had been taken.

Rebecca nodded. "It's lovely. I've never been here before."

"Good. I plan on taking you a lot of places you've never been before." His look told her that he wasn't referring to geographical places but to sensuous places, to levels of pleasure she'd never experienced before.

The rest of their dinner was a hazy blur to Rebecca. Since she'd had only a few sips of wine, she knew that the feeling of intoxication was not alcohol-induced. It was induced by Jake.

After dinner they went on to a popular night spot. Again the lighting was low and the atmosphere romantic. The live music featured a French singer who had a way with torch songs. After her act came a four-piece band. The later it got, the livelier the music got. Soon the handkerchief size dance floor was packed with gyrating couples.

"Let's dance," Rebecca suggested to Jake, who muttered something unintelligible.

"Could you repeat that, please?" she requested over the sound of the music. "I didn't hear you."

"I said I don't know how to dance."

His defensive announcement made her smile. "It's not hard—not to this music and not with this many people dancing. Come on, I'll show you." She took hold of his hand and tugged him to his feet. The unmistakable beat was easy to follow, especially since there wasn't enough room to do more than stand in each other's arms and sway.

"You know, I could get used to this," Jake murmured in her ear. His hands were linked at the small of her back, holding her firmly against him.

"I thought you might like it," she murmured in return.

"I also like this dress. The first time I saw you in it, I wanted to see you *out* of it." Slowly, but oh, so suggestively, he caressed the curve of her back, the inward dip of her waist. Far from protecting her, the supple jersey material of her dress only amplified the slide of his fingers as they neared the gentle curve of her bottom. When his hands tenderly closed on her firm flesh she felt a shock of pleasure clear through her. It felt wonderful, decidedly wicked and very sexy!

She should protest. Her mind wasn't functioning clearly enough for her to figure out exactly why she needed to protest; she only knew she should. But she also knew she wouldn't.

Jake and Rebecca kept dancing, kept swaying, kept touching even though the band had stopped playing. They heard their own music. It was only when the dance floor was almost cleared that they paused, looked around in surprise, then sighed regretfully.

"I guess this dance lesson is over," Jake noted.

"I guess so," she agreed.

Neither one of them wanted to be the first to let go, and reading that fact in each other's eyes, they smiled. A kiss made the parting easier.

They left soon afterward. Once they were in a cab heading back to Georgetown, Rebecca realized that they hadn't done much talking, real talking, yet. Still, they had managed to say so much in silence that it seemed a shame to introduce too many words at this late stage. Besides, the back seat of a cab was no place for a serious discussion. It was a good place for a few stolen kisses, though. Jake had "stolen" more than just a few, with no protest from Rebecca, by the time the cab pulled in front of the de Witt house.

"That's strange," Rebecca murmured. "All the lights are still on." In fact, the place was lit up like a Christmas tree. Rebecca had a sinking feeling that something was wrong, and her suspicion was confirmed when Dorothy met them at the door.

"Thank God you're back!" Dorothy exclaimed.

Rebecca's stomach lurched. "What is it? What's wrong?"

"It's your father." The usually unflappable housekeeper was nervously wringing her hands. "There's been an accident."

Rebecca went cold all over. "Is he all right?"

"I think so, but I'm not sure. The ambulance took him to the hospital almost two hours ago. I tried calling you at the restaurant, but you'd already left."

Guilt flooded through Rebecca. "We went on to a club. Oh, Dorothy, I'm so sorry. I should have called in, checked to make sure everything was all right."

Jake cut off Rebecca's declaration of remorse. "Dorothy, exactly what happened?"

"Bill and I were watching a movie on Rebecca's video machine when we ran out of popcorn. We went into the kitchen to make another batch, and the kitchen ceiling light went out. Bill stood on a chair so he could put a new bulb in. He fell and hit his head on the floor. The paramedics thought he had a concussion, but they weren't sure about internal injuries."

"What hospital did they take him to?" Jake asked.

Dorothy told him.

Then Rebecca asked, "Can you stay here with Amy while I go to the hospital, Dorothy?"

"Of course. You don't even have to ask. I'll stay all night, if you need me. Don't worry about Amy. She's fine. She didn't even wake up when the ambulance came."

"Rebecca, I'll drive you," Jake stated. "Bill showed me where he kept an extra set of car keys."

They went in her father's Triumph. Jake ignored the posted speed limits and drove at what he considered to be a safe speed. Rebecca didn't even notice. She felt numb, yet she was aware that her hands were shaking.

"You know my father got this car when I was sixteen," she said in an unsteady voice. "My brother Kent and I used to tease him and say that it was a more suitable car for us than it was for him." Rebecca lifted one hand to her mouth. "Kent! I should tell him...." She closed her eyes and forced herself to think clearly. "I forgot. He's out of the country on business. He won't be back until next week."

"Calm down. Wait until you speak to the doctor and get some more information; then you can try to reach your brother if you need to. But I don't think it will be that serious. Bill is a tough customer." He took her hand in his and gave it a comforting squeeze. "He's going to be all right."

"He has to be. He just has to be." Rebecca kept repeating the words to herself, over and over again.

When they arrived at the hospital, there was some confusion about Bill's whereabouts. The computer had Bill listed as still being in the emergency room, but the emergency room nurse said he'd been admitted and assigned a room. For once Rebecca was grateful to have Jake take charge of the situation. He not only located Bill's room, but also his doctor.

"Your father suffered quite a fall," the doctor said to Rebecca. "We've been running some tests, but I haven't gotten the results back yet. Until then I won't know the extent of his injuries."

"Will he be all right?" Rebecca questioned.

"We'll know more when we get the test results."

She didn't miss the fact that the doctor had evaded answering her question. "How long will that be?"

"Not too much longer."

"Can I see him now?" Rebecca asked.

The doctor nodded. "But make it brief."

Jake waited outside the room while Rebecca went inside. She came out a few minutes later looking even paler than when she'd gone inside. The brave front she'd put on for her father's benefit crumbled when she saw Jake waiting for her.

"I've never...seen him...in a...hospital...before," she said in a trembling voice. "He looks so...frail." She had to stop and take a steadying breath before being able to continue. "I want to stay until the doctor gets those test results back."

Even though hospitals were not Jake's favorite place—he hadn't been in one since his partner's fatal gunshot wound—he didn't argue with her decision to stay. And he made sure she didn't argue with his decision to stay with her.

They waited in a room that was little more than a cubicle. The antiseptic smell and the sound of squeaky rubber-soled shoes on cold tile floors jarred Rebecca's already strained nerves. She couldn't relax, she couldn't even sit down for very long. She needed to talk, needed to say something to release the tension building inside of her.

"I should have called home after we left the restaurant. I should have checked in, made sure everything was okay. I just wasn't thinking."

"Wait a minute." Jake took hold of her arm and stopped her restless pacing. "You're not blaming yourself for this accident, are you?"

"My own father was being taken to the hospital in an ambulance while I was out dancing!"

"Rebecca, there was no way you could have foreseen what happened. It was an accident. There was nothing you could have done to prevent it."

"Jake, I'm scared. I'm so scared."

"I know you are, honey. I know you are." He took her in his arms and held her tight. "It'll be all right. You'll see." He stood there, just holding her, until the doctor finally returned. The moment Rebecca stepped away, she missed the comfort Jake's embrace had given her.

"Good news," the doctor said. "There don't appear to be any internal injuries. And there's no sign of paralysis. I'm still concerned about possible spinal or cerebral damage, though. Your father received quite a blow to the back of his head. I've got him scheduled for more tests tomorrow."

Rebecca wiped away the tears that welled from her eyes. "Will he be all right?"

"He's in stable condition, but we'll know more tomorrow."

More waiting. Rebecca felt like screaming.

"There's nothing more you can do here tonight. Best thing to do is go home and come back tomorrow," the doctor said.

Jake was glad that the doctor's suggestion was issued as an order, otherwise he didn't think he would have had a chance of getting Rebecca to leave.

Dorothy was eagerly awaiting them when they got home.

"Is Bill going to be all right?" Even though Rebecca had phoned ahead, Dorothy wanted more reassurance.

Rebecca gave it to her. "The doctor said that there are no internal injuries or signs of paralysis."

"That's good. When can he come home?"

Rebecca squeezed her hand. "They'll know more after running some additional tests tomorrow." Seeing the older woman's frown, she added, "Now, don't start getting agitated. Things will seem better in the morning after you've had some sleep. And speaking of sleep, I think you should spend the night here."

"I can drive home," Dorothy stated.

"Forget it." Rebecca was adamant. "You're much too tired to drive. My living room couch converts into a queen-size bed." She started removing the upholstered cushions. "You'll spend the night, or what little is left of it, right here."

"You two seem to have things under control up here, so I'll go on downstairs," Jake said. "Give me a call if you need anything."

"Thanks." The one word couldn't begin to express her feelings, but it was the only thing that Rebecca could squeeze past the sudden lump in her throat.

After she'd gotten Dorothy settled, Rebecca checked on Amy, who was still sleeping peacefully. Wanting to wash off the lingering scent of hospital antiseptic, Rebecca went into the bathroom and took a quick shower. Her classy black dress ended up in the wicker hamper. The blue terry-cloth robe she put on after her shower had been a Christmas gift from her father.

Holding back the tears, Rebecca jammed her trembling hands into the pockets. She needed a soothing cup of tea to calm her nerves, but she wasn't able to face entering the room where her father had been injured. So she quietly let herself out of the apartment and went downstairs to use the main kitchen.

She didn't make it that far. Jake was waiting for her at the bottom of the stairs.

"I thought you'd gone to bed," she said.

He shrugged. "I thought you might not want to be left alone just yet."

"You thought right. How'd you get to be so smart?" she asked in a wobbly voice.

"Just a lucky guess." He smiled at her and held out his arms.

It was the only invitation Rebecca needed.

Nine

The embrace began innocently enough. Jake held her in his arms, offering her comfort as he'd done before at the hospital. He thought it was what she needed. So did she. But soon the need for reassurance was transformed into the need for love. The transition was both swift and startling, surprising them both.

Jake drew back to look at her; she drew back to look at him. Their eyes met. The air between them was heavy with sensual tension, like the electric silence before a storm. Anticipation grew as Rebecca watched his mouth slowly descending toward hers.

Lightning struck when they kissed. His lips claimed hers with gentle fierceness. She not only welcomed his hunger, she matched it. When his tongue evocatively slid past her parted lips and probed her mouth, she responded with seductive demands of her own. She was intoxicated by the taste of him.

One kiss wasn't enough. Not for her, not for him. The darting, erotic interplay between his tongue and hers was a provocative reminder of other intimacies. The undulating rhythm was already underway as Rebecca moved against him. His lips returned to her mouth again and again, fueling the fire, not quenching it.

Rebecca wasn't even aware of pulling Jake into the small rarely used front parlor. She didn't stop to think about what she was doing; she simply wanted this mindless pleasure to continue. As if in a dream she drifted toward the couch. A moment later they were both stretched out on it.

The dynamics of their embrace changed yet again as their closeness took on a new meaning. Rebecca found herself cushioned between the couch beneath her and Jake's warm body on top of her. Wrapping her arms around his waist, she ran her hands over the small of his back. Jake had already removed the suit jacket he'd worn earlier, so all she had to do was tug his white shirt from the waistband of his slacks. Her hands were now on his bare back, his body heat warming her palms.

Jake groaned, lowering his body so that he rested intimately against her. As his leg shifted to settle between hers, he spread a string of kisses across her face. His mouth caressed her temple, the tip of her earlobe, the hollows of her throat. When his progress was impeded by the thickness of her terry-cloth robe, he moved the material aside.

Now he was free to caress the creamy slopes of her breasts, and he did so with fingers that trembled and lips that seduced. Her concentration shattered, Rebecca abandoned her attempts to unbutton his shirt. She couldn't think, she could only feel. Closing her eyes, she tilted her head back and let the pleasure wash over her.

Jake watched her, learning what pleased her, what excited her. The lightest touch to the underside of her breasts made her shiver. She fit into the cupped palm of his hand as if she'd been made for him. Fascinated by the discovery, he brushed his thumb over the rosy tip of her breast. Unable to resist any longer, he lowered his head and continued to work his magic with his tongue.

Rebecca gasped and arched her back. What he was doing to her felt so wonderful. She didn't want it to end. But it did much sooner than she'd anticipated.

With a muttered curse, Jake suddenly heaved himself away from her. He sat there on the edge of the couch with his back to her.

"Jake?" Rebecca's voice reflected her uncertainty.

Even though he knew he shouldn't, he turned to look at her. She was beautiful. With her long, silky brown hair spread out around her she looked like a classic painting he'd once seen in a book. Woman reclining, waiting for her lover. Her lips were slightly swollen from his kisses, and her blue eyes were cloudy with desire. She took his breath away.

He fought the almost overwhelming temptation to take her in his arms again and make love to her the way his body was demanding he should. Jake grimaced. Being noble stunk. But he knew in his heart that Rebecca wasn't ready for this. Bill's accident had made her vulnerable. It didn't matter that she'd been a willing participant. He still felt that he was taking advantage of her, of the situation. And that made him feel like a heel.

While Jake wrestled with his conscience, Rebecca was already coming to her senses. The passion obscuring her thoughts was clearing, and in its wake came a return of her common sense. Amy was right upstairs. So was Dorothy.

Dismayed by how far she'd let her emotions get away from her, Rebecca sat up and hurriedly tightened the robe. She should have been grateful that Jake had called things to a halt the way he had. Instead she felt foolish; she felt inept. *Maybe Jake decided that he didn't want to make love to you after all,* a tiny voice inside of her taunted. Maybe that was why he'd stopped.

But a discreet look in his direction disproved that theory. There was no mistaking the fact that Jake did want her, still wanted her. She desperately wanted to know what he was thinking, yet she was afraid to find out. His words, when they came, startled her.

"I took advantage of you," he said with an old-fashioned chivalry that sat surprisingly well on him.

Rebecca refused to let him take the blame. After all, the responsibility was as much hers as it was his. *She* was the one who'd led him here to the couch. "You did not take advantage of me."

"And do you know why I didn't?"

She shook her head. She had her hopes, but she couldn't be sure.

"Because I care more about you than I care about getting you into bed."

It was what she wanted to hear, what she needed to hear. Her emotions, which had been running close to the surface ever since she'd heard about her father's accident, welled over. So did the tears she'd been holding back all night.

Wrapping an arm around her, Jake pulled her to him. He let her cry, wiping her tears away when she was done, talking to her, reassuring her that everything would be okay. Rebecca rested her head on his shoulder. Listening to the soothing rumble of his voice, she remembered Amy's early description of him as the man who growled like a bear. Other memories followed: Jake finger-painting in the kitchen, Jake handing her that heart-shaped balloon at the zoo, Jake stealing kisses in the back of the cab.

Exhausted from so much emotional upheaval, Rebecca was almost asleep when a realization crept up on her like fog rolling in from the sea. She loved Jake. She silently repeated the words as acceptance settled over her, and she fell asleep with a secretive smile on her face.

Jake stopped talking when he realized Rebecca was sleeping. He carefully smoothed her hair away from her face, awkwardly tucking the strands behind her ear. Her hair was so soft. It clung to his fingers, tempting him to linger. He didn't know how to explain what he felt as he sat there holding her while she slept. It was more than sex, more than passion. He wanted to make her happy; he wanted to protect her from harm.

The way Rebecca was cuddled against his shoulder reminded him of the way Amy had done the same thing when he'd held her at the zoo. But the resemblance ended there. Rebecca was no little girl. She'd responded to his kiss with the full-blown passion of a woman. She'd been so warm, so giving.

He closed his eyes and pictured her lying in his arms again. The sight of her was indelibly etched in his mind. He remembered every detail right down to the way her dark blue robe contrasted against the bared curve of her shoulders. And her breasts . . .

Jake groaned softly.

This wasn't making things any easier. Jake opened his eyes and resolutely channeled his thoughts into deciding how to get Rebecca to bed without waking her. The irony of the situation did not escape him. Here he'd been trying to get Rebecca into bed since he'd first met her, and now he was planning on tucking her in as if she were Amy's age.

As he debated over carrying her upstairs to her bed or carrying her to his bed, the logistical difficulties of both options abruptly presented themselves. Carrying Rebecca upstairs meant getting past Dorothy, who was camped out on Rebecca's living room couch. Carrying her down the hall to his bed meant awkward explanations in the morning.

Jake opted for his bed. He'd worry about where *he'd* sleep later.

Having decided that, Jake slid one arm under her knees and carefully scooped Rebecca up in his arms. He'd barely taken three steps when she woke up with a jolt of alarm. Her movement surprised Jake, who hastily tightened his grip so he wouldn't drop her.

"It's just me," he reassured her as she blinked at him with startled eyes.

Rebecca wrapped her arms around his neck to anchor herself. The floor looked a long way down. "Why are you carrying me?"

"You fell asleep," he explained. "So I was carrying you to bed. The only problem was that I couldn't decide which bed to take you to. Yours is being guarded by Dorothy tonight, and mine will be inspected by Dorothy in the morning."

She had to smile at his slightly disgruntled expression. "Cramp your style, families do, huh?"

"Yeah, but I'm beginning to suspect that families can also bring a lot of joy."

Rebecca didn't know what to say. She savored his words, but so much had happened in the past few hours that she was having trouble even thinking straight anymore. "I'm glad you feel that way." A huge yawn punctuated her words.

"You're beat," he noted with a wry grin. "Think you can make it upstairs by yourself?"

She nodded.

"I suppose that means I should let you stand on your own two feet."

She nodded again, albeit regretfully. A moment later she was standing before him. She paused a second, then reached out to brush her fingertips against his cheek. "Thanks again. Good night."

Jake felt that simple, gentle touch long after she'd left. No one had ever touched him with such . . . such tenderness before. It was as if he'd actually been able to feel how much she cared. And all she'd done was touch his face. Jake was amazed. But then, he'd been feeling that way a lot lately.

Rebecca woke to the sound of the phone ringing early the next morning. She grabbed it on the first ring, afraid that it might be the hospital. But it was just a pushy salesman trying to sell aluminum siding. Rebecca curtly refused and hung up. What kind of person called at 8:15 on a Saturday morning? she fumed.

Considering how worried she was about her father, she supposed it was a miracle that she'd gotten any sleep at all. The five hours she'd been in bed had been restless ones. Now that she was awake, she was eager to get up. She'd barely gotten her feet out from under the covers when Amy shoved open the bedroom door and bounced onto the bed, with Pinkie in tow.

"Morning, Mommy! Wasn't I quiet? Jake betted-ed that I couldn't be quiet, but I was, wasn't I, Mommy?"

Rebecca hugged her. "You sure were, pumpkin."

"Dotty says I can come with her today and visit Micky." Micky was Dorothy's five-year-old grandson, one of the few children Amy felt comfortable with. "Can I, Mommy? Can I go see Micky?"

Rebecca nodded, grateful to Dorothy for coming up with the plan. It meant that she could put off deciding whether or not to tell Amy that her grandfather was in the hospital. Amy was doing so well, Rebecca didn't want to upset her.

"Oh, goodie!" Amy squealed. "I'm gonna go see Micky. Wait till I tell Dotty!"

Amy scrambled off the bed as quickly as she'd scrambled onto it.

"That daughter of yours is turning into quite a little sprinter," Jake commented from the doorway, after having moved aside in order to avoid getting run over.

Rebecca didn't know what to say, so she said, "Good morning."

"Good morning." Jake noticed that she didn't bother putting on either her glasses or a robe to cover up her nightgown. Did that mean that she felt at ease with him or that she was just too worried about her father to bother?

"Where's Dorothy?" Rebecca asked. Keeping to prosaic subjects helped her avoid remembering the discovery she'd made about her feelings for Jake last night. She might have accepted the fact that she'd fallen in love with Jake, but she hadn't gotten used to it yet.

"Downstairs in the kitchen," Jake answered. "She made a big breakfast and then sent me up here to come get you."

"Tell her I'll be there in a minute."

Actually it took her fifteen, but that was because Rebecca called the hospital after getting dressed. Visiting hours weren't until noon. Meanwhile the nurse claimed her father had put in a good night and was currently having another test done. She suggested calling back in an hour.

Rebecca was only able to pick at her breakfast. Not even a basket of Dorothy's homemade blueberry muffins could tempt her appetite. After Dorothy and Amy left for Arlington, Rebecca and Jake went out back to the patio. Although it was still early, the day was already warm. But instead of resting in the shade on one of the white patio chairs, as Jake did, Rebecca began pacing.

"This waiting is driving me crazy," she muttered.

Jake, who'd been noticing the tightness of her jeans and how well she filled them, reached out to tug her down onto his lap. "Just sit still for a minute, will you? You're making me dizzy."

To Jake's surprise, Rebecca threw her arms around him and hugged him. "Have I thanked you for being here?"

"You've thanked me."

She sighed and gave in to the urge to lay her head on his shoulder. "I'm no good in a crisis. You are."

"If you think this is good, stick around. It gets better."

"I'm counting on it," she murmured in reply.

The sound of the phone ringing prevented Jake from responding. Rebecca leaped off his lap to answer it. The call was for Bill. Rebecca took a message and hung up. Checking her watch, she realized that fifty-seven minutes had gone by since she'd called the hospital. She dialed the number again.

This time there was good news. Her father was doing so much better that they'd upgraded his condition to good. The CAT scan they'd done upon admission had been read, and the results were normal. Her father would probably be released in a few days. After speaking briefly to her father and promising that she was on her way to visit him, Rebecca returned to the patio to relay the information to Jake.

"He's going to be all right!"

Jake returned her smile. "I told you he would be."

"He wants me to bring him his bathrobe, slippers and that juicy mystery he's in the middle of."

"Sounds like he's back to his old self."

When Rebecca entered her father's hospital room later that day, she didn't think he looked "back to his old self" yet. But he did look better than he had the night before.

"I brought the things you asked for."

"Good." Bill smiled at her. "Where's Jake?"

"He dropped me off and went to find a parking space."

"I'm glad he's looking out for you. I knew he would."

"How are you feeling?"

"I've felt better. I'm dizzy, but the doctor said that's to be expected. My CAT scan was normal, though. That's a relief. I told them that since they were taking pictures of my brain, I wanted to order a couple extra wallet-size copies for friends and family.''

With that quip, she knew her father was getting back to normal. The relief was overwhelming. Rebecca blinked away the tears.

Bill patted her hand. "Don't tell me you were worried about me? I'm one tough cookie."

"That's about what Jake said." She sniffed.

"He's right. He often is, I've found."

Rebecca mulled over her father's words as Jake drove her home early that evening.

"Bill seemed in great spirits," Jake noted. "I think we should celebrate his recovery."

"I'm not really in the mood to go out," Rebecca said. After the events of the past twenty-four hours, she felt as if she'd been through an emotional wringer.

"Who said anything about going out? We can celebrate at home." Strange, Jake thought to himself, how much appeal that word, *home*, had for him since meeting Rebecca. "I've already arranged everything."

Indeed he had. After sidestepping her curious questions, Jake pulled in front of a small restaurant.

"Stay here," he told her. "I'll be right back."

He left the Triumph double-parked while he ran inside. When he came back he refused to let Rebecca peek at the bags of goodies he carried with him. The smell was enough to make her mouth water.

The wait was worthwhile. Half an hour later, she and Jake were eating—among other things—the most delicious chicken piccata she'd ever tasted, and all in the privacy of her own living room. Jake had unpacked his bag full of goodies and spread them out on the coffee table, which he said he preferred to the conventional dining table. This way he and Rebecca could sit side by side with their legs tucked under the low table.

The proximity made touching inevitable, both above and below the table. Her leg brushed his; his shoulder nudged hers. The distant sound of thunder seemed to echo the growing awareness between them. The approaching storm outside wasn't the only one brewing. Another storm was brewing—between them, sparked by each touch, each look.

The thunder got louder, the lightning brighter, their heartbeats faster. Just as they finished eating, the lights went out.

"Ah, perfect timing. It helps when you've got friends in high places," Jake declared.

"I don't like the dark," Rebecca declared in return.

"No problem." Her comment sparked his imagination. "How about a little romantic candlelight? Where do you keep the candles?"

"I don't have any. I worry about Amy playing with matches, so I don't keep any candles or matches in the apartment."

"What about downstairs?" Jake asked.

"Dorothy keeps a box of matches on the top shelf in the laundry room."

"Ah, the laundry room," he murmured with fond memories.

"But she doesn't keep any candles. We'll have to make do with flashlights. I've got lots of those."

"Not exactly what I had in mind, but it will have to do. Where do you keep the flashlights?"

"There's a small magnetic one stuck to the refrigerator door, and the others are in the tool chest under the kitchen sink."

"You stay here. I'm more used to getting around in the dark than you are." Having said that, Jake got up and proceeded to hit his shin on an end table.

"Are you okay?" Rebecca asked in a worried voice.

"Great," he muttered. "I didn't really need that leg anyway."

Timing his movements to the flashes of lightning, Jake made his way to the kitchen without further mishap. He returned with an armful of flashlights, which he set in a few strategic locations, creatively aiming them up at the ceiling. That way they cast enough light to softly illuminate the room.

"There, is that better?"

"Much," Rebecca replied.

He returned to her side. "So you're afraid of the dark, huh?"

"I'm not afraid of the dark," she denied defensively. "I just don't like it. There's a difference."

"The best thing to do when you don't like something is to concentrate on something you do like."

"Like what?"

"Like . . . dancing."

"There's no music."

"That didn't stop us before. But if you're going to be a stickler about it, I happened to find a portable radio in your kitchen." He held it up for her inspection. "Let's see if we can find something appropriate."

With the radio tuned to music from the Big Band era, the coffee table moved aside and the oval area rug rolled back, her living room was magically transformed into a ballroom.

"Before we begin, we need to take precautions," Jake announced. "Take off your sandals."

Her first thought was that by precautions he meant birth control; she'd heard of various methods, but removing shoes wasn't one of them!

"Go on, take them off," he repeated before leaning down to remove his own shoes. Wriggling his sock-covered toes he said, "This way I won't be afraid of stepping on your feet."

Rebecca was no longer afraid. She was no longer uncertain. Tonight was the night. She felt it in her soul, in her heart and in the innermost recesses of her body. The time had come. They were here all alone in the house. She loved him. He cared about her. It was enough.

Now that the moment had arrived she wanted to savor every step of the path they were traveling. She took off her sandals and held out her hand. "Let's go slowly," she whispered.

Jake knew she wasn't just referring to their dancing. "Slow it is," he whispered back.

The long summery skirt of Rebecca's dress floated around her legs as they danced. Their shadows, cast onto the ceiling by the muted lighting of the flashlights, magnified their movements. Step by step they ventured further; neither leading, neither following, both sharing.

Rebecca relished being in Jake's arms. She felt so secure, so safe, yet so tempted. She gave in to the urge to run her fingers over his back. The dark cotton shirt he was wearing carried the warmth of his skin.

Jake pulled her even closer, erasing even the merest hint of distance between them. He could feel her breathing, feel her heart beating. He stopped dancing. His right arm still circled her waist, while his left hand clasped hers in the traditional dance hold.

"Feel what you do to me." He moved their entwined hands to his chest, positioning her palm directly over his heart.

"Feel what you do to me," she whispered in return, shifting their hands from his heart to hers.

"Rebecca." He transformed her name into a sexy invitation.

Still holding her hand, he used his index finger to tip up her chin so that he could kiss her. His lips claimed hers with unmistakable hunger. A passionate need flared within her, like a match that had just been lit. The time to go slowly had come to an end.

Their kisses reflected their increasing passion. So, too, did their caresses. Rebecca resented his shirt for getting in her way. She didn't want anything between his skin and hers so she separated his shirt buttons from their respective buttonholes. Unlike last night, this time she was successful in her quest.

Jake was equally successful in sliding her dress's spaghetti straps off her shoulders. As quickly as his hands uncovered her, his lips were there to greet every inch of newly revealed flesh. The hollow of her throat, the curve of her collarbone, the slope of her shoulder—all were treated to tantalizingly intimate kisses. Left with no means of support, her dress drifted to the floor, leaving Rebecca clad in a thin cotton teddy.

Jake forced himself to pause. "Are you sure this is what you want?" His voice was raspy, his face etched with desire.

She gave him a sultry smile that almost blew his mind. "I'm positive."

Taking him by the hand, she grabbed a flashlight and led Jake to her bedroom.

"When is Amy coming back?" Jake remembered to ask.

"Tomorrow morning. She wanted to stay over in Arlington, and I said yes."

There was little talking after that. The few clothes they had remaining were quickly dispatched. The flashlight, again aimed at the ceiling, supplied a pale light, barely enough to see by. For once Rebecca didn't cringe from the darkness, but rather felt cloaked by it. Jake took the first step, moving into the circle of light. Rebecca slowly followed suit. He looked at her, she at him, both in awe of what they saw.

"Perfect," he murmured.

"So are you," she whispered softly. She touched him hesitatingly at first, then with growing boldness as he urged her on with words of encouragement. Her questing fingers moved down his chest to his waist and back up again. His skin was smooth and warm. She could feel the flexing of his muscles, the uneven tenor of his breathing. She counted his ribs and tested his self-control. As her explorations became more adventurous, Jake groaned and tumbled her onto the bed, cushioning their fall with his body.

Rebecca's ensuing laughter was gloriously provocative. Jake captured the taste of it, of her. Her mouth greeted his eagerly. She gasped as his hands cupped her breasts. He used his previous knowledge of what pleased her, recalling the exact touch that made her shiver.

But the heated caresses were only a prelude to the magic of his mouth. With his lips, his tongue, his teeth, he wooed first one breast and then the other. All the while his hands were drifting lower, closer to the place that ached to be touched. When he finally touched her there she thought she'd go crazy with the pleasure of it.

As the movements of his hands and mouth became increasingly erotic, Rebecca's pleasure kept intensifying. She felt as if she'd been born for this moment, and she couldn't wait for it a second longer.

"Jake...now...come to me now," she gasped.

"Precautions," he muttered. This time he meant it. He rolled away from her for a few moments.

She welcomed him back with open arms. "Now?"

"Now."

He kissed the words from her mouth, and as their lips merged, so did their bodies. He joined himself to her slowly, giving her time to adjust to him. It wasn't necessary. He'd aroused her so fully that she was more than ready for him. Eagerly, wantonly, she welcomed him, enveloped him, taking all that he had to offer. Her body was sultry and slick as she matched his rhythm.

Jake varied his movements, rocking against her, creating a fabulous friction. Rebecca couldn't breathe, couldn't think. She was unprepared for this glorious feeling building within her. Each gliding thrust, each deep possession heightened the satisfaction and brought with it the promise that the best was yet to come.

It started with tiny tremors that spiraled into pulsating waves. Then the moment arrived like the shattering of glass. In the throes of ecstasy, Rebecca bit her lip to stop from crying out. But Jake's hoarse words freed her from that last restriction. The sound of her breathless moans filled the room, triggering Jake's release. His muffled groan blended with her last panting sigh.

In the hazy aftermath of their lovemaking Rebecca found herself nestled against Jake's shoulder. There were no words to describe how she felt, so she didn't say anything, except for a softly whispered "Wow!"

It came out sounding like a contented purr.

Jake was silent so long that she lifted her head from his shoulder to look at him. "Are you still awake?"

He nodded, his hands combing through her tousled hair with loving tenderness. And then he said the last words she ever expected to hear. "Marry me."

Ten

———

What did you say?" Rebecca shakily asked.

"You heard me. Marry me." He held a lock of her hair in his hand and gently rubbed the silky strands between his fingers. "Now that I've found you, I don't want to let you go."

Jake didn't speak of love. Surprisingly Rebecca wasn't worried about the omission. Knowing his background, she could imagine how difficult saying those words would be for him. But he'd already shown her that he loved her in a hundred little ways. She just hadn't expected things to escalate so rapidly.

"Well, what do you say?" he prompted.

"I don't know what to say."

"Say yes. If you're worried about being rushed, don't be. We can have a long engagement, say...two weeks."

"You'd better be kidding!"

"About the two weeks, yes. About wanting to marry you, no."

"You really think you're ready for a step like this?" she asked him uncertainly. "Marriage is a serious move."

"I realize that."

"It's just that this is all so sudden."

"I told you before that I wanted to settle down," he reminded her.

"What made you ask me now?"

"If all prospective husbands have to go through this interrogation, it's a miracle any marriages take place at all," Jake grumbled good-naturedly.

Rebecca propped her elbow on his chest and, resting her chin in the palm of one hand, proceeded to study him through narrowed eyes.

"What's the matter? Are your contacts bothering you again?" he questioned.

She shook her head. "I'm just trying to figure you out. And you haven't answered my question. Why ask me to marry you now? Because we made love?"

"Because I want to marry you."

"That's no answer."

"Then how about this? Meeting you has changed me. The more you let me into your family circle, the more I realized I wanted the same things you do—a family, stability, roots. I want a woman who has her priorities straight, a woman who's capable of making a commitment and sticking to it. Do you recognize those words? You should. They were the ones you used the first time I told you I wanted you. You said we wanted different things. Maybe we did then, but we don't anymore."

"Jake, there are a lot of things to consider here. I wouldn't just be answering for myself, I have to think about Amy. I'm part of a package deal, and if I marry you, Amy

comes with the package. I've got to think about what's best
for her. The man I marry would not only be my husband,
he'd have to be Amy's father as well. And I can't help wondering if you know what you'd be getting into. Raising a
child is a big responsibility.''

"I've been doing a lot of thinking about Amy myself,''
Jake confessed.

"You have?''

He nodded. "You know, it's funny. When that woman at
the zoo asked me if Amy was my daughter, I had the
strongest urge to say yes. The truth is that Amy's maneu-
vered her way right into my heart. I was a goner from the
minute she offered to share her finger paints with me.'' He
looked at Rebecca with unmistakable directness. "I want to
become Amy's father, and the father to the other kids I hope
we'll have. I know it's a big responsibility, and it's one you
may have to help me with at times. I haven't had much experience at being a father. But I want to learn.''

"Oh, Jake!'' She threw her arms around his neck and
hugged him.

"Did I say something wrong? You're crying!''

"You said everything right.''

"Well? Are you going to answer my question?''

Rebecca knew she should think about it. But she also
knew that thinking about it wouldn't change her answer any.

So what should she do? Let the mistakes she'd made in
the past stop her from moving into the future? Say yes, say
no, say maybe?

"Come on, Rebecca.'' As he often did when he felt at a
loss for words, Jake hid his feelings beneath a layer of humor. "You're not making this very easy on me. In case you
can't tell, I've never asked a woman to marry me before, and
the suspense is killing me. What else can I say? I'll be a good
provider. I'm making enough with my writing to support

you and Amy. I'm in good health and have all my own teeth. You can continue working if you want. Have I left anything out?''

"You haven't said anything about the way you feel about me," she gently pointed out.

"Probably because I've never felt this way about anyone before," he admitted. "You make me feel...I don't know...*complete* is the only word I can come up with. Not very romantic, I know. *Love* isn't a word I've had much experience with. But I trust what I feel for you. I want you, I care about you, I respect you. I know what we have will last."

"*Love* isn't a word you have to be afraid of, Jake. Like fatherhood, I guess I'll just have to help you out with it."

"Does that mean you'll..."

"Yes, I'll marry you."

"When?"

"There's no hurry, is there? I'd like time to get used to being engaged before we get married."

"You're still afraid of being rushed, aren't you?"

She nodded.

He turned her face up to his. "Then we'll go slowly...."

But going slowly was easier said than done, as they soon discovered after telling Dorothy and Bill about their engagement. Bill gave them his blessing and bombarded them both with questions for which they didn't have answers: When were they getting married? Where were they getting married?

"Give me a while to get used to being engaged first," Rebecca replied.

Dorothy insisted on throwing them an engagement party as soon as Bill was out of the hospital and back on his feet.

"We'll need to get a guest list together as soon as possible," she told them.

From past experience Rebecca knew that trying to stop Dorothy once she was in "party-planning mode" was harder than trying to stop a speeding locomotive. There was no use even trying. And an engagement party did sound kind of nice. She hadn't had one when she married Ted; there hadn't been time.

But Rebecca was most concerned about Amy's reaction. She'd already decided that it would be easier if she approached the subject during a strictly mother-daughter discussion.

"Is Jake going to be my new daddy?" Amy asked after Rebecca had broken the news.

"Would you like him to be your new daddy?"

Amy gave the question serious consideration before saying, "He knows how to make monsters go away."

Rebecca nodded.

"And he tells me stories," Amy added.

"That's right."

"And he makes neat aminal noises."

Rebecca smiled.

"I think he'd make a good daddy," Amy decided very judiciously.

"I agree with you," Rebecca said. "I think he'll make a very good daddy." Providing he allows himself to be, she silently tacked on. Opening up was still very hard for him. She was hoping that with enough time and practice, he'd find it easier to express his feelings.

With Bill's release from the hospital, the household soon returned to normal. Unfortunately that meant Jake and Rebecca were in the unenviable position of having no opportunity to repeat their lovemaking. Their abstinence after tasting the fruit of passion was wearing on their nerves, to say the least.

"This kissing you good-night at your apartment door is driving me crazy," Jake muttered on Friday night, one week after Bill's return home.

"Me too," she admitted as he nibbled on her earlobe. "We've hardly had any time together since we announced our engagement. And next week will be worse. My brother Kent is flying in."

Jake groaned. "We've got to speed up our search for a place of our own to live."

"Houses out in the country are hard to find."

"Affordable ones are, anyway." Jake was making good money with his writing, but he wasn't in a position to shell out $1.5 million for a house. Yet that's what houses were going for, at least houses with the amount of land he wanted. He felt stifled living in a city, particularly *this* city. He wanted a lot of space around him. And his failure to find some place to live was getting on his nerves. He'd had no idea looking for a house would be so complicated, or so time-consuming—time that he'd rather be spending alone with Rebecca.

He told himself that his restlessness was caused by his desire for Rebecca. Once he made love to her again, things would get back on track. This feeling of being overwhelmed by it all would disappear.

"Listen, how does spending six hours locked together in a hotel room sound to you?" he asked her.

"Are you serious?"

"Painfully." He moved against her. "Can't you tell?"

"When?" she asked in a breathless whisper.

"Tomorrow. I've booked us a room." He named the hotel where they'd first met.

"Jake, it sounds lovely, but how can we get away? My father's not up to watching Amy overnight yet and Dorothy's family has gone down to Florida for two weeks, so Amy can't stay there overnight either." It went without saying that she couldn't ask Dorothy to stay overnight and watch Amy while she went out and spent the night with Jake. Flaunting their activities like that just wasn't Rebecca's style.

But Jake had already taken all those objections into consideration when he'd come up with this plan. "We won't be gone overnight. We'll go to the hotel at noon and check out the same evening."

Her eyebrows lifted. "What are you suggesting?"

"What does it sound like I'm suggesting?"

"A little afternoon delight?"

"A lot of delight," he corrected her. "What do you say?"

"You mean we would just walk into a hotel in the middle of the day and rent a room?"

"That's the first step, yes."

"But what about luggage?"

"You won't need any," he assured her with a wicked grin.

"Everyone will know why we're there."

"So what?"

"It sounds so...decadent. I've never done anything like that before."

"You did something like that in your bedroom exactly thirteen nights ago," he reminded her, "and the memory of it has been driving me crazy ever since."

"Me, too."

"Okay, then we can do this one of two ways. If the thought of checking into a hotel with your fiancé and no luggage in the middle of the day embarrasses you..."

"It doesn't," she decided. "Actually, now that I think about it, it sounds very appealing."

"How appealing?"

"I'll show you tomorrow when we get to the hotel."

And so she did, but first they had to get past the front desk. "Did you see that funny wink the desk clerk gave us?" Rebecca demanded as they rode the elevator up to their room.

"You're imagining things," he assured her. Jake was having trouble keeping his own imagination in check. He wanted her so badly he could hardly think straight.

The first thing he noticed when they entered their room was the bed—it was huge. And next to it stood a silver ice bucket with a bottle of champagne in it.

"I didn't order champagne," Jake said.

"I did," Rebecca replied, somewhat nervously.

"Nice touch."

"I'm glad you approve."

Now that they were actually in the room, Rebecca felt a little on edge. What she needed was something to break the ice, like a glass of bubbly.

"Why don't you go freshen up," Jake suggested. "I'll open the champagne."

Rebecca walked into the bathroom, only to find it filled with a dozen balloons—heart-shaped balloons! Jake must have arranged this. The thoughtful gesture erased her nervousness. She turned to find him anxiously watching for her reaction. He didn't have long to wait.

She gave him one of those sultry smiles that he'd die for and began unbuttoning her pink blouse. She slid out of it with all the finesse of a stripper.

The lavender-colored camisole she was wearing struck a chord in Jake's memory.

"I believe you once told me that you liked this," she murmured seductively. "I thought you might like to know that it's part of a matching set."

Jake watched spellbound as she kicked off her shoes and stepped out of her skirt. The tiny lavender bikini she was wearing did indeed match the camisole, as did the lacy garters holding up her stockings.

Now that she had his undivided attention, Rebecca reached over to pull one of the balloons out of the bathroom. She then carried it to Jake, who carried her to bed. He never did get around to opening the champagne.

The next time they surfaced for air, it was three in the afternoon.

"Was that your stomach growling or mine?" Rebecca questioned in a languid voice.

"Mine, I think," Jake answered. "What are you doing?" he demanded as she sat up and reached over him.

"I'm calling room service. Man does not live by love alone," she loftily informed him. "Yes, I'll hold," she said into the phone receiver.

"Umm, and I'll hold, too," Jake murmured, doing just that with his hands on her bare breasts.

"Jake!" Her voice rose as he drew her down so that he could taste her with his lips, his tongue.

"Mmm, you taste better than any appetizer."

Rebecca hung up the phone and concentrated her attention on Jake. She seduced, he ravaged, and together they reached a breathtaking climax.

But while Rebecca lay sleeping, Jake brooded. He'd just made an alarming discovery. He didn't simply want Rebecca; he *needed* her, the way a man needed air to breathe and water to drink. And even worse, his need for her was greater—not less—each time he made love to her.

He was losing control of his emotions, something he couldn't allow to happen. Wanting and needing were two different things. Wanting he could handle, needing he couldn't. *It made you too damn vulnerable*. There was a part of himself he had to keep private. It was the only way he knew how to deal with the guilt that had been eating at him since his partner had been killed.

Abe. Jake closed his eyes. He could still see every detail of the funeral as if it had taken place only yesterday. The solemn crowd, the smell of damp earth, the anguished look on the face of Abe's widow, Gloria. Jake flinched at the memory. He'd wanted to approach Gloria then, but he'd hung back, unable to even offer her his condolences. The words just wouldn't come; they were lost in the void that grew between him and everyone around him. By distancing himself, Jake had regained control over emotions that had almost threatened to ruin him. And he'd kept that distance until he'd met Rebecca.

She'd changed him. She made him want things he'd never wanted before, been afraid to want before. Which was all fine and good, providing he kept his wants from becoming needs. Anything else was unacceptable.

Rebecca had no way of knowing that the desperation with which Jake made love to her that afternoon was a warning that something was wrong. As it was, she found out another way.

The argument came three days later. Preparations for their upcoming engagement party were already under way. After work she'd stopped at the studio of an old photographer friend of her father's. He'd offered to lend her his proof book overnight, so she could get ideas for an engagement photograph. The announcement was going to be placed in the newspaper, and she'd thought an accompanying photo might be nice.

Since Jake had said he'd be too busy writing to come to the photographer's studio to look at the proofs, she'd brought them home to him. She'd been trying to obtain

Jake's opinion all evening, but he was proving to be most uncooperative.

"What do you think of something like this?" She held up the proof book for his approval.

He shrugged.

"Okay, what about this one?" She turned to another page and held it up for his inspection.

Jake didn't even look at it. "It makes no difference to me," he said for the eighth time that night.

Rebecca sighed. "Jake, we've got to reach a decision about this tonight. Otherwise there won't be time to get an appointment with the photographer and get the portrait back by the date the announcement has to be put in the paper. So come on, which one do you like better?"

"I told you it makes no difference to me." His voice was curt with impatience.

She closed the book. Obviously they weren't going to get anywhere with making a selection tonight. "Okay, what's wrong?"

"Nothing."

"Then why are you acting like this?"

"Like what?"

"Like you could care less what arrangements I make for the photograph, or for the rest of the party for that matter."

"It's your party, not mine."

"Jake, it's *our* party."

"The party was your idea, not mine."

"What's that supposed to mean?" He was being deliberately antagonistic, and Rebecca felt her control slipping. "If you didn't approve of it, you should have said something before this. The invitations are going out tomorrow!"

"When have I had a chance to say anything? You've been so wrapped up in all these stupid arrangements that I hardly get to see you."

His unfair accusation stung. "That's not true."

"So you're calling me a liar now, are you?"

Her temper flared. "What is your problem?" She'd tried to be patient, but Jake had been baiting her all evening. In fact, he hadn't been acting like himself for several days now, ever since they'd returned from their idyllic afternoon at the hotel.

"What makes you think I'm the one with the problem?" he demanded.

"Listen, I'm not the one who's been cold and uncommunicative the past three days."

"Maybe you should think twice about marrying someone you think is so cold and uncommunicative," Jake retorted bitterly.

"Maybe I should," she shot back, before getting a hold on her temper. This wasn't the way to handle things. "What are we really arguing about here?" she quietly asked him. "Because it's not the photographs, and it's not the engagement party. You're just using those as an excuse to pick a fight with me, and I want to know why."

Her direct approach only made things worse. Now Jake felt cornered. He stared at her with brooding eyes and didn't say a word.

"Don't you think I have a right to know what's going on with you?" Her appeal wasn't working, she could see that. Emotionally he was retreating, distancing himself, and that scared her. She wanted to scream at him, to tell him not to do this to her, to them.

"Talk to me!" she finally yelled at him in frustration.

Silence.

"Are you getting cold feet or what?"

She prayed that he'd deny it. He didn't, and that fact filled her with dread. She read the truth in his eyes. He had the look of a man who'd gotten in over his head and was searching for a way out.

Rebecca sat down before she fell down. This was her worst nightmare come true. *Admit it,* she told herself. *Ever since he first asked me to marry him, there's been a little part of me that's been afraid this might happen.* A leopard can't change its spots, and Jake had been a loner almost all his life. His transformation into a family man had been too good to be true. Yet she'd have staked her life on his integrity. There was something going on here that she didn't know about. There had to be.

She gave him another chance. "You told me that you'd found what you wanted, yet you seem determined to ruin things between us. Why? It's almost as if you don't think you deserve to be happy."

"Stop trying to psychoanalyze me," he ordered in a voice she'd never heard him use before. It chilled her to the bone.

"If that's the way you feel, then maybe we'd better just call this off right now."

"Maybe we'd better," he agreed, killing her last hope. Without saying another word, he got up and walked out of her apartment.

Rebecca wanted to call him back, but what could she say? If Jake didn't want to marry her, there was nothing she could do. So she sat there with tears running down her face, hanging on to the stupid consolation that at least he'd walked out on her before he'd given her a ring. This way she didn't have anything she'd have to return to him. He, on the other hand, had walked off with her heart, and she despaired of ever getting it back in one piece.

An hour later Jake had packed his bags and moved out, with the engagement ring he'd bought her still hidden in his suitcase, the box unopened.

Eleven

Rebecca was determined not to let Jake's departure destroy her. She'd get over it, she'd get over him. She'd survived bad times before and come through. But those bad times hadn't hurt as much as this did. And when the sleepless nights started accumulating, and her spirits continued to nose-dive, she knew she was in trouble because she also knew that Jake wasn't coming back. Three days. He'd been gone three days.

She was still shell-shocked at how quickly everything had come apart. There were times when she didn't accept it, when she was unable to face the fact that she and Jake didn't have a future together. Those were the times when she'd bury herself at work, taking on extra projects, pushing herself to clear up backlogs.

Her behavior was soon noted by her co-workers.

"The Library of Congress may be acquiring material at the rate of ten items per minute, but that doesn't mean you

have to try to catalog them at that speed," Marian Jacob
said. Her kindly pat on the shoulder was enough to brin
tears to Rebecca's eyes.

"Allergies," Rebecca mumbled, dabbing at her eyes wit
a Kleenex. "Happens every summer."

Marian gave her a doubtful look but made no furthe
comment.

Rebecca hadn't told anyone at work about her engage
ment, and now she was grateful for that fact. She didn'
know what had made her wait—some inkling of doubt
some semblance of self-preservation, maybe. But at least a
work there were no pitying looks, no false joviality, no be
wildered questions. She'd had her share of those at home
The only reference to Jake had come yesterday from Nanc
Simon, who'd innocently asked, "Is Jake Fletcher stil
staying with your father?"

"No, he left," Rebecca had answered. Three simpl
words that caused a rift in her heart the size of the Grand
Canyon.

Rebecca marked her success rate in hours, not days. Two
hours without thinking about Jake were hard to come by.

Every time she put in her contact lenses, or took them out,
she remembered Jake eyeing her in the elevator the first time
they'd met. Every time she closed her eyes, she saw his face.
The few times she had fallen asleep at night, it was only to
dream of him.

Her family rallied around her, trying to help her in her
hour of need. But they were at a loss to explain Jake's be
havior. Bill still couldn't believe what had happened and
held out the hope that Jake would soon come to his senses
Dorothy offered to use her rolling pin to knock some sense
into Jake.

But Amy was the one who was hurting almost as much as
Rebecca was. The little girl couldn't understand why Jake

had gone away, and she cried because she thought it was something she'd done. In those moments, Rebecca came close to hating Jake for putting her daughter through this torment. But how could she hate a man who'd thought to leave a shiny whistle for Amy, with the instructions that she was to use it to scare away the monsters if they should ever come back?

Rebecca couldn't figure him out. She wished she'd never met him, and then in the next instant she wished he'd come back. Her emotions seesawed from anger to despair.

What had gone wrong? Had Jake ever really loved her, or had that just been wishful thinking on her part? Maybe he was the kind of man who wasn't able to make a commitment to anyone. But then why had he asked her to marry him? Why had he said that he was ready to settle down, to build a future with her, to be a father to Amy? Had it really all been too much for him to handle?

"He's a louse," Rebecca told Dorothy, five days after he'd left. The two women were downstairs in the kitchen, preparing a pot of stew for dinner. Rebecca was chopping vegetables as if she were a samurai warrior. The poor carrots and celery sticks didn't have a chance. But it was the onions that really got her going. "He's a low-down, no-good jerk!"

"That's right, he's a jerk *and* a louse," Dorothy agreed, before handing her a handful of Kleenex to wipe away her tears.

"It's the onions that are making me cry," Rebecca maintained. "I'm not crying because of him. I've cried enough because of him." She sniffed into the Kleenex. "Where's Amy?"

"Your father's keeping her busy in the study. Go ahead and have a good bawl if you want. You've earned it."

The tears fell more frequently now. "He's a no-good jerk, and I'm well rid of him."

"Sure you are," Dorothy said.

"He's nothing but a playboy."

"That's right."

"He's rotten."

"To the core," Dorothy agreed.

"No, he's not." Rebecca was crying in earnest now. "That's the trouble, Dorothy," she wailed. "He's not rotten. A rotten man wouldn't have given Amy that whistle to protect her from monsters, he wouldn't have gone out shopping half the night looking for a replacement for Pinkie."

"So he was good to Amy," Dorothy allowed.

"It wasn't just Amy." Rebecca remembered the bathroom full of balloons, the gentle kisses, the way they'd made love. "He's a good man with a great potential to love. What happened to him?"

Halfway across town Jake was wondering the same thing himself. What had happened to him? He'd had everything he'd ever wanted right within his grasp, and he'd let it go. No, that wasn't quite right. He hadn't just let it go—he'd deliberately thrown it away. For what?

The words Rebecca had said to him kept returning again and again. "It's almost as if you don't think you deserve to be happy."

She'd hit the nail on the head. Deep down he didn't really feel he deserved all the happiness he'd found with Rebecca. The gut-wrenching truth was that deep down he didn't even feel that he deserved to be alive while Abe was dead. He'd finally faced that fact in the early hours of the morning. He couldn't sleep anyway, so he'd sat up, nursing a half-empty bottle of whiskey and contemplating what he was doing with his life. It wasn't a pretty picture.

Ever since Abe had died, Jake had been running from himself. Like Amy's monsters, he'd locked his feelings into a mental closet and let them fester there. It was time they faced the light of day. And it was time he faced Abe's widow.

He'd called her just a couple of minutes ago. Gloria had sounded surprised to hear from him. And so she should be, he hadn't been in touch with her since Abe's funeral. But he needed to talk to someone about Abe, and Gloria was the only one who would understand. His initial hesitation at discussing what might well still be a painful subject for Gloria was dispelled by her candor. Gloria brought up Abe's name first, and in the course of her animated conversation she let Jake know that she was getting on with her life. She also invited him over for dinner tonight. The old Jake would have refused, the new Jake accepted.

As soon as Gloria opened the door of her small suburban home, Jake knew he'd done the right thing in coming. There was no accusation in the warm brown eyes that looked at him, no placement of blame.

"Well, it's about time." Gloria hugged him. "How have you been?"

Jake lied and said he was fine, although Gloria's look said she didn't believe him.

He was surprised by how much the two kids had grown since he'd seen them last. He'd been to Abe's house for dinner several times in the six years they'd worked together. He remembered kiddingly accusing Abe of trying to convert him into a family man. With that memory came a realization he'd blocked out until now—his first taste of what being part of a family meant had originated here.

As soon as dinner was over, Gloria herded the kids off to do their homework and led Jake into the relative privacy of the living room.

"Okay, now that we're alone, why don't you tell me how you *really* are?" Gloria suggested as she handed him a cup of coffee.

"You always did have a way of seeing right through me."

"So did Abe. Do you remember the time we planned that surprise birthday party for him and Abe caught on right away by the way you deliberately avoided talking about his birthday?"

"Avoiding things seems to be a habit of mine," Jake noted in a voice laced with self-directed anger. "I've avoided coming to see you, or even calling you, for way too long. I'm sorry about that. I should have made contact sooner."

"Why didn't you, Jake?"

"Guilt," he answered bluntly.

"But there was nothing you could have done to prevent Abe's shooting. It wasn't your fault."

"I'm not saying it was. But the fact remains that I'm alive and Abe isn't." And therein lay the heart of Jake's problem. A part of him had always felt that he should have been the one to die, not Abe. No one would have missed him. No one needed him the way Abe's family needed Abe. Yet another part of him was relieved and glad that he hadn't died, glad that he'd gone on to write, glad that he'd met Rebecca. Those two opposing forces, his guilt and his relief at being alive, were tearing him apart. "It should have been me, Gloria."

"Jake, don't even think such a thing! Abe wouldn't have wanted you tormenting yourself like this. He would have wanted you to be happy."

Jake shook his head. "You know, it's funny. I'm successful. I had everything I ever wanted. And I blew it. I panicked because I wasn't in control."

"There are some things we can't control, Jake," she said slowly, as if it were a lesson hard learned. "And Abe's death was one of them. Some things we just have to learn to accept." She paused a moment, giving him time for her words to sink in. "Now tell me what you think you've blown."

Jake did tell her. About Rebecca, and Amy, and his case of cold feet.

"Did Abe ever tell you that he did the same thing when we were engaged?"

Jake shook his head in disbelief. Abe? Mr. Family Man? With cold feet?

"That's right, he called it off two weeks before the wedding. All the preparations, all the responsibility, it suddenly hit him like a ton of bricks, or so he told me. I was ready to hit him *with* a ton of bricks! Luckily he came to his senses the next day, and the engagement was on again. Bridal jitters aren't limited solely to brides, you know. Getting married is a big step. But it's a step you should make based on what you want out of life, not on what you think you do or don't deserve. What's happened in the past can't be changed. Don't let it ruin your future."

"Guilt isn't that easy to get rid of."

"Don't you think I know that? Don't you think I felt the same kind of guilt at being alive, at moving on with my life? I know what you're going through, Jake, believe me. You see, I..." Gloria paused self-consciously, before rushing on. "I've begun dating again. I've met someone...he's very nice. The kids adore him. It's too soon to say whether or not it will get serious, but I'm going to give it a chance. Does that surprise you?"

Jake shook his head. "Not really. I hope things work out, you deserve to be happy."

"So do you, Jake. And it sounds to me as if Rebecca can make you very happy. Don't let that slip away. Needing someone, loving someone, doesn't make you vulnerable, it makes you strong. Loving Abe made me strong, strong enough to go on without him when I had to. But you don't have to go on without Rebecca. You can have what you want, Jake. And you don't have to feel guilty about having it. You've earned the right to be happy. We both have. There's been enough pain. It's time to go on."

For the first time since the shooting three years ago, Jake felt absolved. It was as if someone had stripped away the distorted glass through which he'd been viewing the world and now suddenly everything was clear. He knew what he had to do.

Bill noted the time on the grandfather clock in the hall while on his way to answer the front door. It was after 10:00 p.m. Who could be ringing the doorbell at this late hour? One look through the door's small beveled glass window told him that it was Jake. Bill opened the door.

"Where is she, Bill? I've got to talk to her!"

Bill had never seen Jake so emotional. "Rebecca isn't here, Jake."

Jake stared at him, trying to judge if Bill was telling him the truth. "Then where is she?"

"I don't know."

"Would you tell me if you did know?" Jake challenged him.

"I'm not sure I would. You hurt her badly, Jake."

"I know that," he said in a voice that was quietly anguished. "And I regret that more than you'll ever know."

Seeing the remorse on Jake's face made Bill ask, "Why did you do it? What went wrong? Did I play matchmaker and push too hard?"

"It wasn't you. It was me," he wearily admitted. "There were some things about my past that I had to get straight in my own head. Things that I thought I'd worked out, but hadn't."

"You've got them straight now?"

Jake nodded. Determination settled over him. "Tell Rebecca that I need to speak to her." His use of the word *need* was intentional. It was a word he planned on using frequently when referring to Rebecca. "Will you tell her that much for me?"

Bill nodded.

"When do you expect her back?"

"She didn't say. But I'll give her your message, Jake."

"If I don't hear from her tonight, I'll be back first thing in the morning." Having delivered that warning, Jake left. He sat in the car he'd rented that morning, and tried to clear his thoughts. Where should he go now? He felt lost. He hadn't expected that Rebecca would be out this late. Where could she be? Had she gone out on a date?

Sitting out here stewing wasn't doing him any good, Jake eventually decided. He had to be calm when he saw her again, had to explain why he'd acted the way he had. He just prayed she'd understand.

In the end Jake drove back to his hotel. He'd deliberately chosen his modern, chrome-and-glass-filled surroundings in order to avoid any reminders of the old-world hotel where he'd first met Rebecca and later made love with her. Here everything was efficient and impersonal. Even the elevators were fast, quiet and usually empty. Tonight was no exception.

Discouragement settled around him like a shroud. His expression was bleak as he stepped out of the elevator and reached into his jacket pocket for the modern entry card that would open the door to his room.

"Hey, stranger, got a light?"

Jake froze. That voice! He turned and even then couldn't believe his eyes. It was Rebecca!

"What are you doing here?" He could hardly get the words out.

"Waiting for you." And she'd been waiting for him long enough to question all of her reasons for being there at least once. It had been a long night. After crying over the onions, Rebecca had reached a decision. She wasn't giving up that easily. So Jake had gotten cold feet. There had to be a reason. And she wasn't letting him go until she heard his reason.

No more letting him get away with this strong-silent-type routine. They were going to sit down like two reasonably mature adults and discuss it. Because in her heart she truly believed that Jake wanted to come in out of the cold. She hated to think of his being alone.

Of course the down side to her plan was the possibility that she was making a total idiot of herself, chasing after a man who didn't want her—or if he did want her, it was without any strings attached. Maybe he wouldn't even be alone, maybe he'd already picked up one of those glamorous types he seemed to favor before. Rebecca had argued the pros and cons a hundred times already. But she'd phoned every major hotel, found his whereabouts and come anyway.

He appeared to be alone. That was a good sign. And he was staring at her as if she were the answer to all his dreams, or was that a trick of the strange lighting in the hallway? His face looked thinner, the lines around his eyes deeper. Despite that she thought he was the best thing she'd seen in days.

"We need to talk," she and Jake said simultaneously.

"Would you rather talk downstairs in the lounge or here in my room?" Jake left the choice up to her.

She hesitated.

"I've rented a suite," he added. "There's plenty of room."

Room for what? she wondered to herself. "Is there a sitting room?"

He nodded.

That would probably be a quieter place to talk than the lounge downstairs. She just wasn't ready for a discussion to proceed to a bedroom yet. Probably because it would be much too tempting to just throw herself into Jake's arms and forget about everything else. "All right, we'll talk in the suite."

Feeling as nervous as a rookie cop on his first assignment, Jake ushered Rebecca inside.

"I've got a stocked fridge, would you like a drink?"

"No, I'd like to know what gave you cold feet." Oh, great Rebecca, she thought to herself in disgust. Real subtle. Why don't you just hit him over the head with it? "Uh, on second thought, maybe I would like a drink after all."

"What would you like?"

For you to take me in your arms, she thought to herself. Aloud she said, "I'll have a soda if you've got one." Alcohol might calm her nerves, but it would muddle her thinking, and she didn't want to make any more mistakes.

Jake took two cans of soda out of the minibar. Opening one for her, he handed it to her. "Do you need a glass for that?"

"No, I'll drink it from the can."

We're really progressing here, Jake thought to himself in disgust. Exchanging meaningless pleasantries when he wanted to take her in his arms and never let her go.

They each took a sip of the soda neither really wanted and then got down to business.

"Let's sit down," Jake suggested, hoping she'd sit next to him on the couch.

She chose the armchair across from him.

"I'm not quite sure where to begin," Jake said, "so bear with me here." He took a deep breath and began again. "I guess the whole thing goes back to the reason I quit the police force, the reason I left Washington. Abe's death. You see, I never really got that settled. I just blocked it out and refused to deal with it. That proved to be a bad way of handling it because it all came back to haunt me. I know, I know, you're probably asking yourself what any of this has to do with you and me. It's got more to do with me than with you, although you got hurt in the process. And I'm very sorry for that. I never meant to hurt you. Here I told you to trust me and then went ahead and hurt you anyway. The thing is that Abe's death had left me with a lot of guilt. I was still alive, and he wasn't."

"Oh, Jake..."

"I felt that it should have happened to me, you see. It didn't seem right that a guy with a loving wife and family got killed while I, who didn't have anybody, was left to live. You were right when you accused me of not thinking I deserved to be happy. That's exactly what I thought, although I didn't realize it at the time. Anyway, after sitting around and stewing in self-pity, I went to see Gloria."

Rebecca stiffened. "Who's Gloria?"

"Abe's widow."

"Oh."

"I hadn't seen her or been in touch with her since the funeral, but she welcomed me like a long-lost friend. She helped me see that I was deliberately sabotaging my own happiness in atonement for being alive. You see, I'd discovered something about my feelings for you that scared the hell out of me."

"What do you mean?"

"I found out that I didn't just want you, I needed you. Now, the difference between those two feelings may be minimal to you, but they're worlds apart to me. I mean, you were becoming as important to me as the basic necessities of life—air, water, food. I was losing control of my emotions, and that was something I couldn't allow to happen. So I deliberately pushed you away."

Even with his explanation she still wasn't sure she understood. "Why?"

"Because I needed you too much. Because the last time I felt out of control was when Abe was shot. I couldn't control that, and I couldn't control what I felt for you. The two got mixed up in my head. Rationally I knew I wanted to spend my life with you, but emotionally I was still resisting it."

"You weren't ready to make a commitment."

"No, that's not it. The commitment wasn't what scared me. Needing you scared me, but it doesn't scare me anymore. Neither does loving you."

Rebecca's breath caught in her throat. "That's the first time you ever told me you love me," she whispered unsteadily.

"It won't be the last time," he promised her. "I do love you. If you'll just give me another chance. I know it's not easy for you to understand how guilt could have caused such a mess...."

"I know more about guilt than you think," Rebecca interrupted him to confess.

"You do?"

She nodded.

During their conversation they'd both leaned forward. Their hands bridged the short distance separating them; she reaching out to him, he reaching out to her. Their hands touched. Jake entwined his fingers with hers, gripping her hand with desperate yet gentle strength.

"There's something I haven't told you about Ted," she admitted. "I've never told this to anyone before, not even my father, but I went to see a divorce attorney the day before Ted was killed in a car accident. So believe me, I know how powerful guilt can be, and how it can affect you in ways you don't anticipate. It took me a long time to stop blaming myself."

"I think it's time we both stopped looking back and started looking forward," Jake murmured raggedly.

"I agree."

Using his free hand, he reached into his jacket pocket. "I've got something I've been meaning to give you." He pulled out the jeweler's box. Flipping open the lid, he held out the most beautiful engagement ring she'd ever seen, a diamond surrounded by sapphires set in the shape of a heart. "Do you like it?"

"Jake, it's gorgeous."

"Will you wear it? Will you still marry me?"

"Promise me something first."

"Anything," he said simply.

"Promise me that if you start having second thoughts, you'll talk to me about them. Problems don't seem so bad when there are two of us facing them."

"I promise. Now I want you to promise something."

She repeated his word. "Anything."

"Promise me that you'll tell me when I'm doing something wrong and call me on it. Promise me that you'll tell me what you want, what you need."

"I promise, starting now. I'd like you to put this ring on my finger."

He did.

"Now there's just one more thing I really want," she said.

"What's that?"

"You."

With that he took her in his arms and kissed her. The softness of his lips, the possessiveness of his embrace, expressed what had been left unsaid. That he'd missed her, that he never wanted to be without her again. Rebecca responded with silent messages of her own. The caressing touch of her hands, the warm pliancy of her body, told him she'd forgiven him his human frailties and loved him all the more for sharing them with her.

Not content to simply kiss her lips, Jake spread kisses from her temple to her chin. As if making up for lost time, he murmured his love for her over and over again. Rebecca could have wept from sheer joy. She was back in his arms again. This was where she belonged. Just as he belonged within the circle of her arms.

She touched his face as if reassuring herself that he was real, that this was real. Her fingers traced the line of his jaw, noting the raspiness of his skin. Her lips skimmed his ear, his cheek, his throat. He tasted better than the finest wine and was infinitely more intoxicating.

"I thought I'd lost you," she confessed in a husky whisper.

"Never." He buried his face in her thick hair and rocked her in his arms. "You'll never lose me," he muttered against her ear. "I went to your house looking for you tonight. You weren't there, and I was devastated. I thought *I'd* lost *you*."

"Jake, I love you so much."

"And I love you." He leaned away to give her a crooked grin. "You're right, it does get easier each time I say it. I may never stop."

"Don't." She nuzzled her nose against the open collar of his shirt. "I don't want you to stop."

"You sure you're not going to get sick of hearing me say I love you?"

"I'm positive."

He kissed her again and then set her free, while he was still able to. "What time do you have to get back tonight?" he asked in a strained voice.

"Not until later."

"How much later?"

"A lot later."

He saw the sultry invitation in her eyes and groaned, "Good, because I didn't know where I was going to get the strength to let you go."

This time his kiss held the full strength of his need for her. This time there was no holding back. He worshiped her with his hands and his body, letting her feel what she'd done to him. They left a trail of clothing from the sitting room to the bedroom. His jacket, her blouse, his shirt, her shoes, his slacks, her skirt.

Rebecca left her more intimate apparel for Jake to remove. He granted her the same pleasure, seducing her with intimate compliments and erotic promises. He reacquainted himself with every inch of her body, returning to those spots he knew brought her joy. Rebecca was equally eager to bring him joy.

Overcome by desire, they sank onto the bed, their bodies slick and warm. He came to her with loving tenderness and awesome passion until they were fully joined together.

Rebecca shivered with delight. "Don't move," she whispered.

He froze. "What's wrong? Am I hurting you?"

"No, it just feels so good that I want to...mmm...savor it."

"How about savoring it this way...?" Jake rolled onto his back, carrying her with him.

Rebecca looked down at him and blinked her eyes in surprise. When he moved, her expression became one of wonder. With Jake showing her the way, it didn't take her long to discover the many advantages of her new position. Pleasure came in increasing steps that brought her and Jake to the peak of satisfaction in explosive harmony.

Cradling her in his arms, he rolled with her again until they both lay side by side. This time Jake was the one who said "Wow!"

Rebecca grinned and ran her finger over his lips. "You don't seem like the kind of man who says 'Wow' very often."

"I'm not. In fact, you are the only woman I've ever said 'Wow' to. No, I take that back. There was one other girl...."

She playfully socked his arm. "Don't tell me about her."

"But you'd like her. She's a lot like you."

"I'm warning you, Jake...."

"Her name is Amy. And I said 'Wow' after she solemnly informed me that you must like me because you even put on makeup for me."

Rebecca smiled. "Ah, makeup. The ultimate sign of affection. What we women put on for our men."

"It's what you take off for your man that I really appreciate." He gave her a wicked leer and ran his fingers down her bare back.

"You've got a naughty mind, Jake Fletcher."

"I know."

"But a very kind heart." She placed a kiss in the center of his chest. "Thanks for giving Amy that whistle."

"Did she have to use it against any monsters?"

"No, thank goodness."

"When she gets older, I'll teach her how to really whistle," Jake promised. "You already know how to whistle, don't you, Rebecca? You just put your lips together and blow."

"You mean, like this?" Her mouth hovered millimeters from his as she licked her lips and then pursed them.

Jake framed her face with his hands and kissed her before she could demonstrate further. "Just like that," he murmured against her mouth.

"Since I already know how to whistle," she whispered seductively, "what else are you going to teach me?"

"The same thing you've taught me. That we belong together."

It was a lesson they never forgot.

*   *   *   *   *

FOUR UNIQUE SERIES
FOR EVERY WOMAN YOU ARE ...

Silhouette Romance

Love, at its most tender, provocative,
emotional ... in stories that will make you laugh and
cry while bringing you the magic of falling in love.

6 titles per month

Silhouette Special Edition

Sophisticated, substantial and packed with
emotion, these powerful novels of life and love will
capture your imagination and steal your heart.

6 titles per month

Silhouette Desire

Open the door to romance and passion. Humorous,
emotional, compelling—yet always a believable
and sensuous story—Silhouette Desire never
fails to deliver on the promise of love.

6 titles per month

Silhouette Intimate Moments

Enter a world of excitement, of romance
heightened by suspense, adventure and the
passions every woman dreams of. Let us
sweep you away.

4 titles per month

SILG-1R

Take 4 Silhouette Special Edition novels
and a surprise gift
FREE

Then preview 6 brand-new books—delivered to your door as soon as they come off the presses! If you decide to keep them, you pay just $2.49 each*—a 9% saving off the retail price, *with no additional charges for postage and handling!*

Romance is alive, well and flourishing in the moving love stories of Silhouette Special Edition novels. They'll awaken your desires, enliven your senses and leave you tingling all over with excitement.

Start with 4 Silhouette Special Edition novels and a surprise gift absolutely FREE. They're yours to keep without obligation. You can always return a shipment and cancel at any time.

Simply fill out and return the coupon today!

* Plus 69¢ postage and handling per shipment in Canada.

Silhouette Special Edition ®

ATTRACTIVE, SPACE SAVING BOOK RACK

Display your most prized novels on this handsome and sturdy book rack. The hand-rubbed walnut finish will blend into your library decor with quiet elegance, providing a practical organizer for your favorite hard-or soft-covered books.

Only $9.95

Approximately 16" x 8" when assembled

Assembles in seconds!

To order, rush your name, address and zip code, along with a check or money order for $10.70* ($9.95 plus 75¢ postage and handling) payable to *Silhouette Books*.

Silhouette Books
Book Rack Offer
901 Fuhrmann Blvd.
P.O. Box 1396
Buffalo, NY 14269-1396

Offer not available in Canada.

*New York and Iowa residents add appropriate sales tax.

BKR-2A

Silhouette Romance ™

Legendary Lovers Trilogy

BY DEBBIE MACOMBER....

ONCE UPON A TIME, in a land not so far away, there lived a girl, Debbie Macomber, who grew up dreaming of castles, white knights and princes on fiery steeds. Her family was an ordinary one with a mother and father and one wicked brother, who sold copies of her diary to all the boys in her junior high class.

One day, when Debbie was only nineteen, a handsome electrician drove by in a shiny black convertible. Now Debbie knew a prince when she saw one, and before long they lived in a two-bedroom cottage surrounded by a white picket fence.

As often happens when a damsel fair meets her prince charming, children followed, and soon the two-bedroom cottage became a four-bedroom castle. The kingdom flourished and prospered, and between soccer games and car pools, ballet classes and clarinet lessons, Debbie thought about love and enchantment and the magic of romance.

One day Debbie said, "What this country needs is a good fairy tale." She remembered how well her diary had sold and she dreamed again of castles, white knights and princes on fiery steeds. And so the stories of Cinderella, Beauty and the Beast, and Snow White were reborn....

Look for Debbie Macomber's *Legendary Lovers* trilogy from Silhouette Romance: *Cindy and the Prince* (January, 1988); *Some Kind of Wonderful* (March, 1988); *Almost Paradise* (May, 1988). Don't miss them!

SRT-1

Silhouette Intimate Moments

NEXT MONTH
CHECK IN TO
DODD MEMORIAL HOSPITAL!

Not feeling sick, you say? That's all right, because Dodd Memorial isn't your average hospital. At Dodd Memorial you don't need to be a patient—or even a doctor yourself!—to examine the private lives of the doctors and nurses who spend as much time healing broken hearts as they do healing broken bones.

In UNDER SUSPICION (Intimate Moments #229) intern Allison Schuyler and Chief Resident Cruz Gallego strike sparks from the moment they meet, but they end up with a lot more than love on their minds when someone starts stealing drugs—and Allison becomes the main suspect.

In May look for AFTER MIDNIGHT (Intimate Moments #237) and finish the trilogy in July with HEARTBEATS (Intimate Moments #245).

Author Lucy Hamilton is a former medical librarian whose husband is a doctor. Let her check you in to Dodd Memorial—you won't want to check out!